MILLER'S REVENGE

ROBERT JOHNSON

Brown Paper Publishing
2010

BleakHouse Reprint Edition
2013

MILLER'S REVENGE

a novel by

ROBERT JOHNSON

cover art & text design
SONIA TABRIZ

cover design
LIZ CALKA

Illustrations by
RACHEL TERNES

BleakHouse Publishing Reprint Edition

ISBN: 978-0-9837769-4-9

Published by Brown Paper Publishing, 2010;
Reprinted by BleakHouse Publishing, 2013

www.bleakhousepublishing.com

Printed in the United States of America

ACKNOWLEDGMENTS

I am grateful to the many colleagues, students, and friends who read and commented on earlier drafts of this book, notably Liz Calka (who also designed the cover and helped with text design), Rachel Cupelo, Samantha Dunn, Kellee Fitzgerald, Charles Hucklebury, Chris Miller, Susan Nagelsen, Shirin Karimi, and Sonia Tabriz. I thank Elmo Chattman and Chris Miller for allowing me to use some of their compelling poetry in this book. (Chattman's poem is clearly labeled within; Miller's poem, *Allure*, forms the basis of a letter that appears on page 119).

I am deeply and especially indebted to my colleague and friend, Sonia Tabriz. Her sharp eye for detail and her unfailing way with words have served me well as I wrote and revised this book. I am grateful to Tabriz, as well, for allowing me to quote from her compelling commentary, *Empty Cell Windows*, and to make reference to her engaging story, *The Prison Librarian* (written with Victor Hassine).[1] As if these various contributions were not enough, Tabriz also created the cover art and designed the text, in both cases with her distinctive sense of style. For this BleakHouse Publishing reprint edition, I extend my thanks to Rachel Ternes, whose vivid and evocative illustrations add greatly to the text and help pull the reader into the story, and to Harmony Jovet, who proofed the text with great care.

---

[1] *Empty Cell Windows* and *The Prison Librarian* can be found in *Lethal Rejection: Stories on Crime and Punishment*, published by Carolina Academic Press, 2009.

CONTENTS

ONE HOT SUMMER NIGHT

The man on the steel table was mine, my client. I work for the dead. I bring them justice. When someone in prison is murdered, I take the case. I'm a murder cop, detailed from the inner city of Baltimore to the cell blocks of the state penitentiary. That's my beat—the prison, the pen, the house, call it what you like. Just be glad you're not there. You might not live to tell about it.

There are 2,500 full-on felons doing time in here, and only a handful will ever see the light of day. And they'll have cataracts and canes by the time they get back to the world. The rest go out in body bags, black plastic sacks with red toe tags. Tags say natural causes, suicide, or homicide. Prison homicides are raw, bloody, hands-on killings. Face to face violence, up close and savage. Torn up bodies in the cells and on the tiers, in the yard and in the messhall. A few in the showers, naked and dead. This one in the gym. Fully clothed but missing one eye, courtesy of his killer.

Murders are called hard cases. That's what's written on each case folder of a murder victim: HARD CASE. In bold letters. Plus the vic's name. The crime goes down and they come to me, Robert Miller. Most folks call me 'Rob'. Suspects call me 'Sir'. Everyone is a suspect until I say otherwise.

Now this case, the murder of Jamal Jordan, was clear cut, at least in the beginning. He'd been killed by Daunte McFadden, who'd pretty much slaughtered him in front of an army of witnesses one hot summer night in an underground gym filled to the rafters with convicts serving sentences so long they might as well have been buried alive.

"Mister Jamal Jordan, Case 102..." The voice, soft and sensual, wrapped in a cultured Italian accent, came floating toward me, impervious to the cool white tiles that covered the floors and walls of the prison hospital basement, a vault, really, doubling now as a morgue, making most speech sound tinny and strained. "Here before me," the throaty, resonant female voice continued, "is the body of a young man, well nourished and apparently healthy, before the assault that took his life."

"Well, Dr. Simone, I ...

"Call me Vittoria, for heaven's sake. And I'll call you Rob. We've had enough cases by now, is that not true?"

It was true, and I was happy to be on a first-name basis with Vittoria Simone, the medical examiner who picks up the prison homicide cases and makes a preliminary determination of the cause of death. We don't exactly work together but we do work side by side. Not as close as I might like, and I'm not alone in that. Vittoria is pushing forty and still turns heads in pretty much any setting. In prison, she's a force of nature.

"OK, Vittoria. Fair enough. He may have been well-fed..."

"Nourished. Well-nourished, Rob. No one in prison is well-fed."

We laughed. Meager portions of barely edible food are a major topic of complaint in the house. Somehow it's enough to nourish a body, a mystery in itself, though not one I ponder much.

"But he is definitely dead now, Vittoria, so what does it matter?"

"Very observant, Rob. Really."

4

Vittoria stretches out her r's in a seductive way; always makes me smile.

"Thanks, I can see he's dead. I'm wondering why you always start with comments like 'healthy young male' or 'well-fed... uh, nourished.' It seems odd, is all."

"I like to remind myself that I'm working on a person, or what was until very recently a person, and often a healthy young person with a long life ahead of him. This Jamal Jordan was a young man, a man whose hands were once held by someone who cared about him, whose lips someone once kissed with tenderness..."

"I take your point, Vittoria," I said, interrupting her, perhaps a little uneasy about the humane sentiments she brings to these cases, sentiments I share deep down but like to keep deep down, out of the picture. I'm also uneasy because I know from working in this sorry prison that there are plenty of men here who've never been loved, some never held with tenderness, even as children. They grow up angry and wild, and end up living – and dying – in cages. "It's a grim business, this dying in prison."

"And the eyes," she continued. "You wonder – I wonder – what memories lay behind them."

Jamal's right eye had been ripped from his head by the force of the attack, evidently with a serrated knife. There was something terribly intimate about this violence.

"What he last saw," I said, "that sort of thing? You wonder about his dying memories?"

"Well, here you have to think that his last sights were truly terrible, maybe violence beyond human comprehension. But mostly this wound is such an insult..."

"A violation..."

"Yes, a violation. And on many levels. His assailant destroyed his life, then violated his memory along with his body."

I nodded, my face reddening with anger. "This man was slaughtered and..."

"I see the tragedy, I suppose, Rob," she said, while gently caressing the victim's hands, "while you see the need for justice."

"Oh, I know. He's there, and he's mine. I work for him."

"So you say, but you are here and the crime scene is not here, yes?"

"Yes." I smiled. "The crime scene is not here. You have a point, Vittoria. I'll mosey on down to the crime scene and let you prepare your report."

"Mosey?"

"Hey, you're from Italy and you don't know from spaghetti westerns?"

I exited with that line, feeling witty and maybe even attractive in a rough, from-the-mean-streets sort of way, grabbing my rumpled, summer-weight cotton sports coat from the coat rack by the pitted, grey steel door, one of a few relics from the day the prison was something on the order of a dungeon for the dispossessed. I'd heard the heavy footfalls of my escort and was ready to get to work.

The officer detailed to walk me around the pen, the man with the big set of keys, came dressed for battle. He looked like a paratrooper or maybe a special operations goon, and I thought I saw some blood on his sleeve and along the outer leg of his bloused-out pants, the bottoms tucked neatly into his shiny prison-issue boots. Of course it might have been sweat stains. We're in the middle of a summer heat wave, sweltering in a prison with windows that don't open and ventilation, of a sort, provided by industrial fans that mostly blow hot air up and down the corridors. There is a stale smell in the air, the congealed odor of lifetimes spent in close quarters with people committed to poor hygiene.

"Officer?" I called the man officer because these guys are called correctional officers. That's their title. But they don't dress for corrections, whatever that means. They dress for war and believe me, prison is war, at least this prison, at least some of the time. Tonight was one of those times.

"Detective Robert Miller? I'm Officer James, Richard Kevin James. I'm here to take you to the gym."

"The crime scene," I replied. I'm direct but my tone was soft, or at least not harsh. He's young, and I see he's shaken up.

"Yes, sir, the crime scene. That's where Jamal Jordan got, well, he got..."

"Cut up pretty bad, I understand."

And I did understand, regrettably. The gym in a maximum security prison these days can be a death trap. A lot of prisons have closed down their gyms. Some prisons are so crowded the gyms have been converted to makeshift housing units. In effect, prisoners are stored there under close scrutiny, living each day on their bunks with no place to go other than the toilets or the showers. More often, the gyms have been shuttered because of killings and even riots that jumped off there, sometimes after hot tempers fanned by competition and other times after well-planned paybacks, done in the open to send a message. I'd heard of one guy chased the length of the gym, then knifed and left for dead, until he got up again and ran some more and was finally finished off by some gangbanger looking to make his bones. You had to wonder who could ever feel safe in the gym these days.

When I started working back in the seventies, the gym was an oasis. Nobody wanted to lose gym time. Or movie time. The movies, offered weekly, were shown in the gym. You could hear a shank drop, it was that quiet, but no one brought shanks or any other weapons to the gym back in the day. Nobody did their dirty work in the gym. My young escort knew none of this. In his time here, the gym was what it was – a jungle – and getting worse by the day.

"Yeah, cut up pretty bad," Officer James continued. "I mean, it was just incredible. His face..."

"I understand, son." The young man was hurting. You could almost see the hint of premature worry lines traced in the full, pale Celtic face he inherited from his ancestors; a face increasingly out of place in prison these days, when our penal institutions house so many African-American men that they sometimes seem like modern day plantations. Or extensions of the ghetto. A lot of convicts see the prison as the next stop in the downward trajectory of their lives, and it's hard to argue with them. Many are casualties of the Drug War, fought out every day on the mean streets of the inner city, decimating many poor black communities. Sometimes I look around me and I'm reminded of the old Richard Pryor joke: "The prison is justice for the black man: just us."

"Take a deep breath," I said. "I take it you witnessed the killing?"

"Well, I saw the end result, you know, the finished deal, the blood..."

"OK, then, we need to talk. Let's start while we walk. First the gym..."

"Crime scene, sir."

I smiled. "Yeah, crime scene, then later the suspect's cell."

James seemed relieved to be walking. He opened up pretty quick. "You know this place, Mister Miller, I know you know – you work here, too, but I work in the trenches, day in and day out. It's hell, man, sheer hell."

An acrid smell had overtaken us as we moved out into the main prison, not fire and brimstone, I thought, but fitting for a place everybody called hell at one time or another.

"Another fire?" I asked, waving my right hand to clear away a thin trail of smoke lingering in the air around my head. I'm resigned to the problem of fires in prison cells, set by convicts in moments of anger or madness, a problem I didn't know existed until I worked behind the walls of this old state prison, dating to the early nineteenth century and equipped with fire hoses that run up the sides of the tiers and look almost as old as the prison itself. You could always tell a new fish when you walked by his cell and saw it stacked high with papers and books and hobby crafts – tinder, when you came right down to it, and sometimes things did come right down to it. Most guys smarten up and keep their cells free of excess stuff, resigned to the hazards of the fire trap they have to call home.

We try to keep the fires down, but there are times that it doesn't much matter what we do. Like New Year's. We're outside in the world celebrating and the cons are inside this curious hell burning down the house. With themselves locked inside. In cages. Makes you wonder. Smells like desperation to me but what do I know? I don't even know why men court so much danger to get to the basketball courts in the prison gym. But they do. And some of them pay dearly.

I've come to accept that fires are a part of prison life, a little like life in Southern California – OK, maybe that's a stretch, but what I'll never be resigned to is the look and smell of a dead body, burned and smoldering in a cell. Some guys burned themselves. That's a pretty effective way to go over the walls, if you could get past the horror. Others got taken out with fire bombs, for reasons good and bad and sometimes for no reason at all. A prison cell is a convict's house, whether he likes to admit it or not. When a cell gets firebombed, it's like an act of terrorism. Domestic terrorism. It's certainly terrifying. And not just for the vic. The screams of burn victims are like nothing I'd ever heard. A full-throated howl, starting deep and getting high-pitched and hysterical. Raw animal panic. Then there's "the charred remains," as our report writing guidelines put it, which often are formed into a kind of skeletal outline of the body. Like a sculpture, done in ash. These are the hardest of the Hard Cases, because everybody on the tier seems to die with the victim and nobody, not staff, not inmates, not anybody ever really gets over it. I smell burned toast and I can be right back in one of these crime scenes. Enough to put you off breakfast for a lifetime.

I never want to hear those cries again, ever. I don't want to examine another toasted corpse. But I will. Just a matter of time.

"Yeah, Mister Miller, a few burns today. No bodies. Just headaches. Heat brings it out."

I puzzled over that for a minute, then asked, "Why's that, Officer?"

"I think heat gets the men crazy. Maybe they figure a little fire will get 'em out of their cells for a bit, you know, a taste of fresh air."

"Or fresher air. Not much nature in this house. They just get put into another cell, usually with two guys already in residence."

"Pretty futile, I suppose, when you think about it," Officer James conceded.

"This fire have anything to do with the crime, Officer?"

"Doubt it. Maybe. Word spreads fast. Anyway, I know some things about this crime you may want to know."

We moved to the side, instinctively, to let a group of prisoners shuffle past, men in shackles on their way to buses that would ferry them to other cages in other prisons. The bus transport company, a private outfit called Charon Express, used their own shackles, replete with a logo suspiciously reminiscent of a skull and crossbones carved into the metal, a sore spot with the men. Convicts bound for the Express were shackled in pairs – awkward for them but efficient for the bus company since the prisoners were secured in units of two in each of the bus seats, the seats in turn nestled in their own wire mesh enclosures. A few of the sad creat-

ures passing by looked up at us but mostly the men moved in slow motion, heads down, slouching under the weight of opprobrium, the sheer force of social rejection embodied in the hardware that held them in place in uneasy alliances, constraining their movements to the prison's version of ballet, a noisy *pas de deux* of short steps on the balls of the foot balanced by cuffed hands swaying from side to side for balance. They were convicts; we were keepers. The bottom line was that we had a life, they didn't. Sour resignation sometimes gave way to raw violence, I knew all too well, but not from men in shackles.

Not usually, anyway.

One man looked back, caught my eye, nodded. I nodded back. I knew the man, and I knew more than I wanted to know about prison buses and their shackled charges, a dull but occasionally risky assignment for staff and, again occasionally, one scary ride for the prisoners. A man had been killed on the Express a few years back. It was Rodriques, Felix José Rodriques who'd

12

caught my eye. He'd been my star witness on that case, and now he was off to a different prison, one with programs and work and school, a delayed but much-deserved reward for his cooperation. Some call it snitching. I call it getting busy and doing the right thing.

Rodriques had wanted to do the right thing. Badly. The first words out his mouth told me he knew what he was talking about. "The chain, man, the chain that held his cuffs to his belt, it made a rasping sound. The dude, the crazy dude, pulled the chain over the kid's head and around his neck, then pulled up, pulled up hard, man, along the back of the seat." Rodriques was visibly upset. "And the guy, just a kid, really, he just gurgled. Gasped. Gurgled. Fucking chocked. I'm not sure but that sound will haunt me, man, does haunt me. I dream about it. Jones, he's known, man, known as a bad ass. He'd pulled the boy's head back, right up against the back of the seat, you know, the rail. And then the sorry sonovabitch *lunged* back, pulling the kid just about up and out of the seat. Surprised his head stayed on, man, that's how hard Jones pulled on that boy. Kid's legs was kicking, he's reaching out, flailing out with his arms. But he couldn't say nothin'. Couldn't get no air. Just gurgling. Choking. Like forever, man. Like it would never stop."

I said, "I see," and I did. Still do, sometimes, when I let my mind wander.

"It did stop," Rodriques continued, "man but it seemed like forever. Still think about it, man."

I nodded, then asked, "And then what happened?"

"And then the kid was still."

"Was there any blood?"

"Yeah, there was blood. Jones' cut him after he chocked him. Used a razor. Saw it on the floor."

"Yeah, we got it. Covered in blood and some sort of...

"Slime," Rodriques added. "Mucous or snot, man. Jones coughed it up, man, spit it up from his throat. He musta swallowed the razor and then spit it up when he needed it. People do that around here. Some people."

I knew this from previous cases but it wasn't something I liked to think about. How do you prevent violence if people go to those lengths to arm themselves? How do you protect yourself, let alone the prisoners? The answer, I knew, was to run safer prisons, but good luck with that these days, when the house is full and bursting at the seams with convicts who might never see the free light of day.

I asked, "And what else was happening during this, uh, assault? Did anybody move or say anything? Or do anything?"

"Nothing, man. We just looked ahead. We're all in shackles. Chains. We can move around a little, sure, but me, I was frozen there."

"Frozen?"

"Afraid, man. Terrified. Just about shit myself. Did piss myself. Yeah, wet my fuckin' pants. Thought I'd be next."

I couldn't blame the man for being terrified and I would've pissed my pants, too. 'Most def', as some of the cons say. I figured it was best to just move on, as if what he was telling me was just ordinary stuff.

"What about the officers?" I asked.

14

"What about them?"

"Well, there were officers in the front and the back of the bus."

"Yeah," he replied, "and that's where they stayed."

"They didn't do anything?"

"Shined a flash light, man. Turned on the overhead light."

"And then what?"

"And then nothing?"

"Let me see if I've got this right," I said, pausing for emphasis. "The officer, or officers..."

"The woman in the front was watching TV, man. TV."

"Watching TV?" This was news to me, but at that point I had a lot to learn about the Charon Express and the hellish ride it provided.

"On her iPod. Or cell phone? Glued to the screen."

"And she..."

"... didn't do shit," he said, angrily. "Had earplugs in. She was gone, man, might as well have been on another planet."

"The officer in the back?"

"He turned on the light, used his flashlight, too. But he couldn't see nothin'. Or didn't see nothin'."

"Or saw something and did nothing?" I added, hoping my growing irritation at my colleagues in the guard force didn't show.

"Your words. That's not me speaking."

"But it's possible?"

"Oh, yeah. It's not like the CO is gonna break up a homicide in progress if he don't have to."

"Because..."

15

"Because he's afraid. Or she's afraid. Or because he or fucking she don't give a shit about us."

"So, nothing?"

"Nothing, nothing at all. "

I knew Rodriques wasn't exaggerating. The bus had about six guys on it when the killing took place, heading back to the house from court. All of them had called home that night to talk to loved ones, to reassure them, tell them they were OK. Or at least alive. The calls were recorded. Routine. The conversations were anything but routine. Hardened cons were scared, depressed, glad to get off that bus alive. The bus was like a nightmare from a Stephen King story, with a real live monster in their midst, taking a man's life with impunity.

Or a boy's life, which maybe made it worse.

"Mom," said one guy when he called home, "dude put the poor bastard's head in his lap, rocked him like a baby."

"He talked to the boy like he was a baby," another guy said. "Told him, 'rest now, little one, it's all right, it's all right.'"

Little one, I thought. How eerie is that?

"I thought the guy had gotten out of his chains," shouted one man into the phone, still very much afraid, "thought he'd just busted loose and we was all food." Food. Meaning dead meat. Even felons have to eat, feeding off the misery of their brothers. He didn't have to explain this to his family – they knew plenty about this kind of misery – but when the case went to trial we were reminded that many people in the real world didn't get this little piece of prison parlance.

"The smell," said another guy, to his wife, or at least his baby mama, I can't recall. "The smell was awful." He paused, and you could hear him swallowing. "Boy pissed himself, and his blood was everywhere. Everywhere..."

"Those guys got a long ride ahead of them," said Officer James when the bus group had been processed and moved, one by one, through the next gate and we were free to proceed to the gym.

Longer than you'd imagine, I wanted to say, still thinking about Rodriques. But instead I said, "You were talkin' about what I need to know? Things I need to know to work this case?"

"Yeah, need to know, whether you want to know or not."

I was starting to like this officer, though I couldn't stop thinking of him as a kid. And kids, I knew, could have it rough in here.

"Like what?"

"Like the gym, where it went down," he replied. "I'll take you there, Detective, tell you a little about what was happening when the violence jumped off."

"I'm listening."

And I was listening. It occurred to me, not for the first time, that folks don't listen much to COs. CO is short for correctional officer, men and women often long on insight but short on respect from others. A mistake, not to listen to these folks. They know this place almost as well as the convicts, who live here 24/7. They get training on how to listen to others; least we can do is listen to them.

"Well, first, you got to know that this was tournament night. A big deal, the gym packed; I mean there must have been a 100 an' some guys stacked up in there. It was so hot you could hardly breathe but people was up for the game, really into the game. The two teams and the rest mostly fans, really into the game."

"Mostly fans? Who else was there?"

"The gym is like a hangout, too, Mister Miller. You know that. There's folks who go for haircuts. The barbershop is right there, right?"

"Yeah, I've seen it. The vic was a barber, right?"

"Right. He wasn't playing that night, far as I know. He wasn't cutting hair, either. Least ways, if he was cutting hair, he must have taken a break 'cause he was out on the gym floor, talking it up with some folks on the sidelines."

"What do we know about him?"

"Well, Jamal Jordan, he's a player. Or was. Not a ball player so much; a player in the black market. He was probably hanging some but also dealing, doing his business."

"Bidness, right?"

"That's how they say it, Mister Miller."

"Right out in plain view. His prison bidness?"

"No, Mister Miller, not like that. Some of the hacks are dirty but most of us, we wouldn't stand for that. Too dangerous. Let people deal out in front like that and things can get outahand."

"So he's trading on the down low?"

"Right, probably in the barbershop. Officers on gym duty can see into the barbershop from the basketball court but you can't see everything. People are moving around, shaking hands, trading cigarettes, you know, a lot of bidness transactions."

"Bidness transactions. You gotta love the language here, don't ya?"

"Yeah, like this is some sort of commercial zone. Which it is, it's just we can't stop it. Really, we'd have to strip search everybody all day long."

"Not a pretty picture."

Prisoner hygiene is a sore spot with staff. Nobody likes to search a man you can smell at ten paces and the convicts don't like it much either – the smells or the searches.

"Jamal's a player, like I said," Officer James continued, "he deals, is what I hear. And I'm thinking he's dealing from the gym."

"Makes sense. Take the product where the action is. So Jamal's out on the floor. What else is going down?"

"Mostly the game. I didn't even notice Jamal, not really anyway, until he went down. I was watching the game."

"Not the action around the game? Not scanning the crowd? This is a hotspot, Officer James." I try to keep the irritation out of my voice.

"I know, I know. I mean, I blame myself, I do. I'm a fan. Anybody who loves basketball and works in prison lives for the tournaments. That night the Masked Marauders were taking on the Fortunate Felons..."

"Masked Marauders? Fortunate Felons?" I thought he was joking. I thought maybe I should get out more, drop in on the action, take the pulse of the place. Listening to Officer James, I was beginning to feel like a tourist.

"Hey, these guys got a sense of humor. They're down but they're not out. Last year it was rap names, like Akon Aces and 50 c..."

I knew Akon, and maybe a few prominent rappers, like Tupac Shakur. One of my sons put an Akon ring tone on my cell, though I'm careful to keep the phone on 'manner mode' when I'm at work. Everybody watches their manners here, where etiquette can be a matter of life or death. People have been killed for bumping into someone else and not apologizing fast enough. Or laughing at the wrong time; someone figures you're laughing at them and takes mortal offense. Somehow the strains of "Locked up, won't let me out; no, they won't let me out" – the main refrain of my ring tone – doesn't strike me as good taste, let alone good sense, when I'm in the house.

"OK, got it. So the Masked Marauders were taking on the Fortunate Felons...."

"The gym was rocking. Place packed so tight you couldn't stick your legs out without getting 'em out onto the court, where they'd like as not get run over. And these guys play for keeps. The place is hot; feelings running hot. What else they got but pride?"

I nodded. This prison, like so many of the old state pens these days, is for lifers. Lifers mostly want a simple life, stay close to home, avoid trouble. A lot of these guys are like displaced Zen Masters. They struggle to stay in the moment, clinging to routine, focused on Now because Before and After are disasters they don't want to face. One guy told me, "I got no memories worth remembering and no light at the end of this stinking fucking tunnel." I could see where getting with the prison routine might

20

help hold his head together. Sometimes we all need to live in a kind of automatic pilot, just not forever. For lifers, it's forever.

But there are a few outlaws in this bunch, lifers who live on the raw edge of emotion. They burn with resentment; hate everything they see and everyone they know. They want to live in *your* moment, and make it a nightmare. Rogues. Like rogue elephants that wreak havoc in the jungle. Rogue lifers make prison a jungle. And with them, everything is personal and everything is for keeps.

"I tell my girl," Officer James continued, "'Baby, we got men doing life, double life, even life plus the afterlife!' Some of these dudes are modern-day desperados, believe it. The game is like a shootout. The winners are legend, least for a while."

"Least in their own minds."

"But the game, man, the games are good, really good. Some of the black prisoners here call it the NBA—Natural Brothers Association. 'We be the NBA,' that's what the guys say."

"So you watch. And you pick a team, root for them."

He paused. He should just be policing the place and we both knew it. "Yeah, I pick a team, I'm a fan. But I just watch and cheer."

"Until somebody gets killed..."

"Yeah, 'cept normally no one gets killed or even hurt during a big game. Maybe a game injury but mostly folks behave because they want to stay to see the action. The action on the court, you know."

"Not tonight, though. Somebody got good and dead tonight, right in the middle of the big game."

"Yeah, not tonight. I was preoccupied. I didn't see it until it was too late. Didn't see it until I heard it."

"Heard it?"

"The silence, Detective. Heard the silence. The place was alive – clapping and hollering and then, boom, silence, dead silence. Literally. Then somebody yelled, 'Man down. Man down.' Down and out, really. By the time Jamal hit the floor, he'd been knifed in the eye – way down deep into his head, detective – and slashed across the face. And as soon as he hit the floor, Daunte kept working at him..."

"You recognized the assailant?"

"Well, I recognized the man, didn't know he was Daunte McFadden 'til later, when things settled down and I checked his number."

"OK, go on."

"So Daunte – you know, the assailant, was cutting Jamal deep in his back and chest and arms. Jamal's hands were cut to shreds..."

"Defensive wounds?"

"That's what I'd say, but he didn't really defend himself; he didn't have a chance. One minute the ball is in play and the next, it's the big time out. Sudden death. Game over."

"Nobody called out or tried to step in, nothing?"

"Nothing, Mister Miller. It was so much blood, I think everybody was paralyzed. I know I was paralyzed. It felt like I was stuck there, it was like the air was thick, hot and thick, like it was syrup – thick as blood – and I was suspended in it. It seemed like time stood still, me like a fucking statue on one side of a river of blood, Daunte on the other. It seemed like he was in a trance, too.

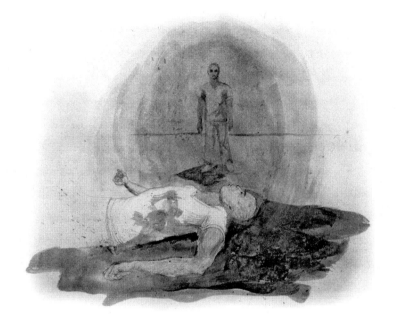

"Take a deep breath," I said.

"I never seen so much blood, Mister Miller, never. Jamal took the hit just off center court, along the sidelines, near the toilets. By the time we figured out what had happened, there was so much blood we was slippin' and slidin' trying to get out there. Daunte, he was drenched in blood, blood from head to foot."

I knew enough from Vittoria to know that Jamal had exsanguinated. In plain English, he'd bled out, right in front of the officer, his heart pumping wildly at first, pushing torrents of blood through expanded veins, him high on adrenaline and fear. Until the body figured out that the blood was draining off into nowhere. Then Jamal would go into shock, a numb, blessed state of indifference or even, in some cases, relief. Vittoria had told me about this, that people who survived profound assault often reported feeling calm, even tranquil, in the face of what should spark raw terror and frantic efforts at escape. The ones who died of such assaults were reported to behave the same way, to look calm, composed, even happy on death's door. "It is as if they give up on the ghost, Rob," Vittoria had said, "and go quietly into the dark night." She paused and added, "that is a play on the immortal words of Dylan Thomas, in the case that you are wondering."

It wasn't the case that I was wondering, but that was my problem. Imagination's never been my long suit. "Or give up and become a ghost," I'd replied, trying to be smart but coming off lame. Vittoria ignored me and observed, "It is a matter of evolution. We have evolved to slow down the pumping of the heart and the expansion of the veins and the movement of the limbs under profound assault. Movement, even fast beating of the heart, in these cases is self-defeating, it hastens death. Better to go into a kind of coma and hope for help."

"And if help is not available?" I'd asked. "Then at least you die in the state of peace," she said, "in a dreamy departure from this life." And a state of grace, I thought to myself, if you were clear-headed enough to make peace with your Maker in those last minutes.

Later, I'd review the crime scene photos and see a pool of blood spreading out from Jamal's body, forming a giant Rorschach design, oddly like that of a butterfly, though on second glance I thought more like a rat – they grow them big in prisons, and in big numbers. The stain was a dark brown bordering on black, and the blood had congealed, as if it were a species of asphalt laced with angry suppurations.

"Did they exchange words?" I asked the officer, bringing us both back to the matter at hand. "Any threats, name calling?"

"Nothing, not that I heard, anyway."

"How about Daunte, him standing there drenched in blood. Did he say anything?"

"No, not a word. Daunte just looked at me. Like he was in shock. Took a few steps back and then stood there, like a fucking bloody statue. So I went to Jamal, you know, to help. He's moving and moaning and I get to him and look him in the eye—the eye that ain't cut out of his head—and all I see is black. Dull, like flat paint. That's what really did it for me. That man was looking death in the face, and God I about dropped dead myself."

"So you're standing there..."

"I'm standing there looking at Jamal, I'm like in a trance or something, and then I hear, 'Drop the knife.' It was a female CO. 'Drop it now!' She's a woman but she has balls. 'Drop it NOW!'"

"And he dropped the knife?"

"Not right away. Seemed like forever. Daunte's standing there, dripping blood like from a horror movie and I'm thinking, 'Or what. Drop the knife or what?' I mean, nobody wanted to go take it from him. We just stood there. We was on one side of a river of blood, and Daunte was on the other, and ain't nobody moving until Daunte drops the knife."

"So he did drop it? You didn't have to take it from him?"

"He dropped it. If he didn't, we would've waited for backup."

"Right."

"Hey, we're not armed. We don't have batons."

"I'm not judging you. I know how it works."

"We do have mace but you don't want to spray that shit in a confined space."

We share a tight smile. It's unspoken but we know that prisoners have been left to die, the whole thing on camera, because officers didn't want to break protocol and go to their rescue. The drill is to wait for backup when a man is armed and assaulting another prisoner. The backup guys come in heavy gear – helmets, stun shields, heavy batons, looking like rejects from some demented NFL league. In some cases they're made to line up outside the area of the violence, and go before a camera, each guy giving his name and position. Jim Jones, Left Leg. Joe Minster, Torso. Like I said, NFL, just a little twisted. The cons get it; No Fucking Luck, that's what they say goes down when these guys get busy. Busy suiting up, mostly. Sure, they get the job done, but usually long after the killer has got his job done, too. And all of this can occur in some pretty tight places, so everybody knows that somebody is dying while some other folks are following procedure, waiting for a backup crew to arrive and follow their procedure.

"Yeah, a confined space. But that gym, that was a real tight place, tighter than a rat's ass. Place felt like a steam bath. You spray mace and all hell would break loose. It'd be a fucking riot."

"So Daunte drops the knife. Then what?"

"Daunte drops the knife and gets down on one knee, like he's a quarterback or something getting ready to call a play."

"Or maybe say a prayer?"

"Didn't seem like he was praying, Mister Miller, but anyway I move up behind him and cuff him, but it's hard 'cause of the blood and the cuffs getting wet and slippery. He helped me, man, really, he did. Helped me with the cuffs! I guess he was spent, no fight left in him."

"Helped you put the cuffs on?"

"Yeah, I couldn't get a grip. First I put them on upside down, so they woulda been a bitch to get off him."

"Christ. And risky. You'd practically have to do contortions to get them off without putting your neck on the line, Officer."

"Damn right. Imagine that? Man cuffed and then chokes me when I try to cut him loose later. Things coulda gotten outahand, man. Somebody'd have a heart attack."

"More work for the paramedics," I said. That's a grim thought but I can't help but believe that this crime scene could've gotten "outahand", to quote this officer, a man who may be lucky he's alive after his shift in the gym tonight.

AIN'T NO CLEAN THING

We walked across the yard, once an open expanse of grass filled with convicts old and young milling about, sometimes hundreds at a time, now subdivided into a dozen outdoor cages, each a little prison of its own complete with a concrete or asphalt floor and thick steel fencing to keep group size down and enemies apart. "It didn't use to be like this," I said to Officer James, in what I meant as a wistful tone.

"Like what?"

"Broken up like this. Like dog runs."

"Hey, don't good fences make good neighbors? Didn't someone say that?"

I was sure someone did and maybe I'd remember later, over a drink – with Vittoria? – but I said, "more like a way to break up trouble before it starts."

"I'd heard people had the run of the yard back, well, what, in the eighties?"

"Yeah, even before that," I replied. "Long before that."

Maybe a century or more before that, I was thinking, but that was a long story and this was a short walk. I sometimes felt like an archeologist or a historian when I walked the yard, taking in the old buildings, imagining why they were built the way they were and why things turned out the way they did. This place was originally a penitentiary – a place of penance. A fortune was spent building it to resemble a monastery; high hopes hung on the belief that criminals could do penance, going straight from the inside out. When that hope died, the place took on a kind of benign indifference to the lives of the prisoners, who were pretty much

31

free to roam the yard at will. The walls were high and well protected, but daily life was turned over to the convicts, who made themselves a kind of community. Now, well, the cons were seen as too dangerous for that sort of thing, as "super-predators" by one expert's reckoning, and so they were locked into little worlds – like the pens in the yard – to hold them in check.

"Really," said Officer James, clearly skeptical. "I can't see how you'd police these guys if they could mingle out here. It would be a bloodbath."

It was the gangs, I knew, that made things different today. And the gangs, in turn, were a last-ditch effort by the convicts to deal with a very punitive system, one so punitive we led the whole fucking world in the prison biz, with our easy resort to incarceration even for first offenders, with our long sentences, and the notion that we put people in prison to get them out of our hair rather than give them a second chance. Or we simply killed them. The death penalty was alive and well in this country and in this prison, which had its own death row and death house. Then there was what I called death by incarceration, my name for life without – without parole, without hope, without mercy. But this all seemed normal to Officer James, who started working at a time when life without parole for teenagers – some of them not yet past puberty – was considered normal.

"Well, I see your point," I said, trying to pick up on some shared experiences, "gangs don't play well together."

"And the old folks," said James, pointing to a fenced in yard off to our right, "boy they'd be sitting ducks!"

"About all they do is sit around," I replied.   In their institutional wheel chairs, I thought to myself, or in walkers, which did make them easy targets, though I knew of a guy who used the arm of his chair as a club, and a formidable one at that.

"This is new too, you know?   Old folks in prison." I was starting to feel like an old guy who gives out canned wisdom whether the audience wants it or not. "Old folks, or at least so many of them, doing hard time. And kids who work them, beat them, even rape them." You don't know sad until you interview an aging, broken down man whose just been thrown out of his wheelchair, raped, and then had his ride smashed to bits. Men age fast in here, and that's on the good days. Most days are full of fear and anxiety, which can age anybody, fast.   A wave of gray humanity was about to engulf our prisons, this I knew from training. The cages were looking better and better.

We passed The Home, the name for a series of pens reserved for the old and infirm, the worst of them staring off into space, seemingly fixed in place, like catatonic refugees from an insane asylum or worse, figures stuffed and mounted in a museum. These were the ones who clearly were grounded for life. At times when I walked this part of the yard I thought I'd wandered into an old age home in a very poor country, "No Country For Old Men," I thought, calling to mind the title of a book by the great Cormac McCarthy, a popular writer among some of the cons. One of my favorites, too. Only this sorry home was filled with illustrated men, sagging tattoos stretched and distorted on each human canvas, hate and lust and violence the major motifs. If prison has its cautionary tales, they were to be found in this enclave of cages, "geri built," as one officer put it, for the geriatric felons, many slated to die behind bars. I wasn't sure who had it worse. The young men slaughtered by other young men or the old men who died neck deep in waste and decay, crying out for their mamas long dead and gone.

Vittoria had a soft spot for these guys, our senior citizens. She'd linger over their bodies, tenderly. "I try to mourn for them, Rob," she'd once told me. "Their lives were long and empty and painful. You can see the neglect etched into their features, like cracked statutes left out in the way of the elements. Very sad."

I knew the details of some of those sad lives and tried not to dwell on them. But it was hard. One of the guys we passed came into prison a reasonably healthy man at age 50. I thought he nodded to me, but his head may have simply lolled forward, onto his chest. He was 60 now, not so old in the world but really getting on in prison. In the ten years he'd been down, he had nine strokes and two heart attacks. His carotid arteries were rotting away to nothing. Vittoria knew his story, told me there were many like him here, out there, on their own, vulnerable. Some days the man couldn't hold a conversation. Seems a doctor who didn't speak much English – that's most of them in here – gave the man meds he was allergic to, then thought his patient was malingering when he got sick. A sorry excuse for a home, like I said.

The young guys these days have their own sad stories, often told in the language of tattoos. Inked up good, these guys. We're talking gang tats, set off by gang colors, when they could find clothes in gang colors, mostly reds and blacks, and a few variations on sport's team uniforms. The Raiders were a favorite;

34

no surprise there, I suppose. No sags on the taut flesh of these gangsters, some of them by rights mere children, but some ugly scars might break up the body art. It's not unusual to see a man with a deep necklace scar, like someone tried to slit his throat all the way around. Some of those neck cuts are deep, like the man almost got his head cut off. It's an everyday thing to see scars running across a man's cheek, stitched up rough in the infirmary. Tattoos dress these guys up a bit, I guess, and many sure need it. Convicts did tats back in the day, but now tattoos are called body art and they're everywhere. It's hard to find skin without a tattoo, or without several layers of ink, new tats used to cover old, maybe a few times over. Cover up job for those scars, too. I had the impression that the prisons were becoming a world of their own, out of touch with the mainland and proud of it in a bitter, fuck-you-for-forgetting-me kind of way. It was like prisoners divided themselves into lost tribes, committed to staying lost. Like that show, *Lost*. Convicts used to come back to civilization, or at least want to come back. The guys gave up on us when we gave up on them. When I look at all the spilled ink in the pen, I see despair and it makes me a little sick.

We arrived at the squat stone building that holds the gym, walking the last bit in silence, lost in our own thoughts. We paused – always good to stop and reflect before you enter any new setting in the house – then went down a few steps to the entrance, which is underground. A painted sign, bathed in grime and amended by fresh graffiti, was displayed above the gym door in bold letters. Originally, the sign had read "House of Hoops." Somebody in the rec department had thought that up back in the seventies. A

Lakers fan, not that it much matters. Not too long ago, judging by the fresh look, it had been altered to read "House of the Hopeless." The original sign was in black paint; the editing, as it were, was in bright red. It made an impression.

"House of the Hopeless?" I turned to engage my escort, who knew a lot about basketball, maybe especially prison basketball.

"Hoops, then Hopelessness," he replied, in what I can only call a tone of meditation. "I guess basketball is life but not enough life for the men. Like I said, these guys are doing forever. I don't think one of the guys in the gym tonight will leave the prison alive."

"Certainly one didn't. So the sign is what, Officer, something from literature, 'Abandon all hope— '"

"Beats me. Maybe they've been abandoned by hope."

I replied, "I see," but I'm not sure I did. Until he opened the door.

First thing that struck me was the smell, then the army of naked men, clothes at their feet, blood on the floor, a hint of rot in the air. Even the crime scene tape was smeared in blood, looked sticky to the touch; as if the "Do Not Cross" warning was futile, that the whole gym would soon be overrun by the spreading blood. I do crime scenes, that's my job, but this looked like a massacre, the men like refugees, the overall effect like some sort of "end of days" scene from the middle ages.

"Christ, gimme that clipboard."

Officer James grabbed the clipboard hanging by the door of the gym and handed it to me. It was the gym log. Everybody in the gym was signed in. Nobody would be signed out until I said so.

With one exception. Jamal Jordan had a pass. He'd been released to the coroner, and his body was in the gentle hands of Vittoria Simone. Something, I thought, some small consideration, though I knew this fleeting pleasure was lost on Mister Jamal.

"Alright, Officer," I said, forgetting Vittoria and getting my mind back in detective time, "you've been a big help. Before I start working on these guys, I want to know if you asked Daunte about the crime or if he made any incriminating statements."

"Well, I didn't interrogate him, if that's what you mean. It's more like I yelled at him, you know, I was pumped up. I said, 'Why'd you do this man, you crazy or something?' I didn't know Daunte, 'cept by sight, but I know Jamal. Knew Jamal. This is a small world."

"And Daunte said?"

"He just stared at me. So I screamed at him, really loud man, 'Why'd you do this man, you crazy or something?' I was feeling tight man, ready to explode. And you know what that stupid bastard told me? Daunte said, 'I ain't supposed to be here.' Like that's a reason."

"I ain't supposed to be here," I repeated. That was original, I had to give Daunte that. I'd heard, "It wasn't me" or "I wasn't even there," but "I ain't supposed to be here?" That was something new.

"I'm going to start with the man at the head of the line, Officer. When I'm done, I'm going to see Daunte McFadden."

"Right, sir. The first man is..."

Crime scene interviews can be an empty ritual in prison. The killing could take place on a raised stage in the prison yard and nobody'd see a thing. But you've got to try, and sooner or later you might catch a break. If there are enough eye witnesses, a few of them will figure they need a favor in the bank. They talk to me, I remember them, maybe cut them some slack down the road. Maybe. There's no guarantees in here; I do what I can. But there's always trouble down the road, so getting on my good side is not a bad insurance policy. It's the way it works in here. As one of the old cons once said, before fingering his cell mate, "Investigation in the joint ain't no clean thing."

So we all get a little dirty, if we're lucky. This was one of those times. After a series of brief encounters of the uninformative kind with a few heavily tattooed convicts who claimed surprise that a killing had occurred that night – one man went so far as to opine that the ocean of blood filling the gym was from a game-related injury – I talked to a guy named Danny DeLeon and started to get somewhere.

DeLeon was doing life for murder, his third. He didn't want to go into the details of his crimes and I didn't either. He told me he was in the gym office "getting cups for the players." I must have looked interested because he went on to explain, "I'm the main water boy." I resisted the temptation to ask about subsidiary water boys. I did think the boy in this guy was long since departed, maybe with his first homicide. I kept that thought to myself.

"Anything at all you can tell me, Mister DeLeon?"

"The word on the street is that it was a hit."

"A hit? Daunte hit Jamal?"

"No man, not like that. Word was that *Daunte* was going down. Dude called Snake supposed to do it."

"This Snake have a name?"

"Beats me," he said, shrugging his shoulders. "I just heard Snake. Snake was the man." DeLeon paused, then said, softly, "Hit men don't have real names, Detective."

That last line sounded like the title of a B movie or the first line of a *noire* novel but I didn't see much to be gained by saying so. Instead I said, "So nobody knows the hit man called Snake?"

"I didn't say that. Maybe someone do. But I don't know him, least not for sure."

"There a lot guys named Snake in here?"

"More than you'd imagine, Detective. This is a regular reptile house."

I nodded. The man had a point. I sometimes imagined the cons slithered around each other, heads poised, bodies tensed, ready to attack. Mostly show, of course, but enough to keep your guard up.

I pressed a bit, figuring DeLeon knew more about this particular snake than he was saying, but he must have figured he'd said enough. I've got to accept that. It's not like we're at Guantanamo Bay or I'm a card-carrying Republican who thinks critics of water-boarding are all pussies. I can't beat it out of him, not that a beating would do any good. It's all talk in the interrogation biz, but a man has got to feel safe enough to open up. Most don't, and I can't blame them. It's not like we could protect them if the chips were down. You could ask Jamal Jordan, though of course it was a little late for that. "Thanks for coming in," I said, then motioned for the next man.

That man was Darnell Ross, a double lifer who told me he was sent up for murder and aggravated rape. I hadn't asked, but since he brought it up, I wondered for a minute if the aggravation was the killing or if the vic aggravated him so he killed her. His crime may have been brutal, even savage, but he mentioned it almost casually and I couldn't help but notice that he looked relaxed, like he was at home. "I was getting my hair braided, man," he told me. I took this in stride. You see a lot of this in prison, like the pen's a beauty school for men who've seen only the ugly side of life. "Looks good," I said. He nodded. I was glad he didn't ask, "Compared to what?" These guys don't scare me much anymore, but I have good sense.

"Ever hear of a dude named Snake, a prison hitter?"

Ross just got up and left. Not so much as a "fuck you" on the way out the door. I thought maybe this Snake business might be real. A loose clue, because nobody got killed but Jamal and sure enough he didn't get killed by a hit man; Jamal got killed by Daunte, that much was certain. But I thought I'd look into this Snake character, if I could get some traction on his real name.

Jermaine Wilson swaggered up to my table, which had been set up in the barber shop area, near the general toilet. Accommodations are often crude in prison. I mention Wilson's swagger because he was naked down to his boxers, as were the others after they'd been strip searched and allowed to get back into their shorts, the prison's concession to decency. It takes character to walk with confidence in your shorts in the middle of a murder investigation in a maximum security prison with the smell of blood still hanging in the air.

"I use the 5th," Wilson said, getting to the point. I didn't bother to make him specify "the Fifth Amendment" or say anything about self-incrimination. I wasn't asking him to incriminate himself, as far as I knew, but I dropped the matter, since it was clear he'd have nothing to say. I tilted my head to the right, keeping my eyes locked on his. He strode back to the line, looking like he felt vindicated.

The next convict was an angular white guy, who fixed me with a stare that suggested he was really intense or maybe a little demented. I didn't know there'd been a white guy in the gym that night, but there he was, sitting erect, looking at me without blinking. He struck me as part military, part weasel. Head shaved, beaklike nose, pronounced Adam's apple. A couple of biker tats; no Nazi stuff, least that I could see. Which makes sense when you consider that he was the sole white guy in the place, the proverbial needle in a haystack of angry black felons who'd eat white racists alive. Not that I normally notice these things, but the guy looked like what my mother would have uncharitably called "white trash." I didn't figure him to know much but smiled anyway, hoping for the best. He did come to me, after all, and I was there to talk.

I asked, "So, what can you tell me?" My tone was firm but friendly, I thought.

"I can tell you my name," he replied. After a pause, he continued. "And why I'm here." Another pause. "Oh, and what makes me, uh, special. But I bet you already know."

I smiled more broadly. This was feeling a little like show-and-tell in kindergarten. Or on the mental ward.

He took my smile for an invitation to go on.

"My name is Markowski. Alan Stanislaw Markowski."

He paused.

I said, "And..." And waited, figuring he'd fill in the blanks, as promised.

"And what?" he replied.

"And what are you here for, for starters?"

"I'm surprised you have to ask?"

"I'm surprised you didn't tell me. Didn't you say you'd tell me why you were here? And what made you special?" My smile was fading. I thought he must have been a pain in the ass, even as a kindergartner. Or a patient. Or maybe a mentally ill kindergartner. This guy might have been a whack from day one.

"Well, I figured I wouldn't have to tell you. You'd just know."

"Why the fuck..." I paused. "Pardon me." I generally contain my anger in these situations. Keep things professional. "Why would you think that, Mister Markowski?" I asked, regaining my bearings.

"Because, well, my name's been in the papers. I'm something of a legend, you know."

I didn't know, and legend or not, this was clearly a waste of time. I'd had enough. "Well, thank you for coming..."

"No, wait. Really, hold on. I'm the guy who killed all those girls? Buried them in my mother's backyard? Then buried her there, too. You didn't read about that?"

I could see his feelings were hurt. Back to that kindergarten thing again, although the mental health angle was still prominent in my thinking.

"You really don't know who I am?"

"I don't, I'm sorry." I couldn't believe I was apologizing to this clown. "I'll read up on your case."

"And that I escaped from jail a few years back, using bed sheets from the laundry? That's when I got to kill my mom. I hated to do that but I hated her, you know?"

I didn't know, but I imagine she hated him, for sure.

"She helped the cops. Fuck her. That's how I figured it."

The escape and the killing of his mother, called the 'mama drama' in the tabloids, brought the crime back to me but I wasn't going to give this guy the satisfaction.

"I'll check it out. Thanks."

"You do that. And man, I didn't see nothin' tonight."

I noticed he said nothin', not nothing. He was talking tough, resetting his head to go back into the jungle. I didn't like the sonuvabitch but it did occur to me that his life here might be a special sort of hell.

"Nothing?" I said.

"Not a fuckin' thing. I keep to myself. Just wanted to..."

"Introduce yourself?"

"Yeah, let you know there are some real criminals – smart criminals – in this shithouse full of niggers."

"OK, Markowski, back to the playground." Hard time or not, crazy or not, this guy was where he belonged.

The next prisoner spoke to me through gritted teeth, like he was an extra from a Jimmy Cagney movie, not that he'd ever seen a Cagney movie – the kid looked about twelve. (Looks can be deceiving; I later learned the kid had killed a guard, so he had some weight in the pen.) "It was jive hectic," he told me – a few times, before I heard it right. At first I thought he was saying "electric," which made sense, sort of. It certainly was shocking, even for this place.

"Electric, huh."

"Hectic. Jive Hectic. Crazy."

"Yeah, things were crazy in there?"

"Insane, man. Crazy insane." He spit the words out though clenched teeth, the left side of his lip lifting just enough to let the strained sounds find space to bloom.

I wasn't sure what to make of this guy, whose name I couldn't understand but whose face looked familiar. It was a haunted look I'd seen before, and then it came to me. I'd been investigating a killing near his house. This guy lived in a corner cell on the flats, not far from where a body had fallen in a heap, the head crushed, the face smashed beyond recognition. It was awful, he'd explained to me, patiently, enunciating with great care, as if speaking to a child, but not unexpected. This sort thing happened in his neighborhood. "This ain't no Sesame Street," he'd told me, in a more normal tone. The bad thing is the scream. This particular guy didn't scream because he was dead before he was pushed off the tier. But another guy had screamed "like a bitch" at the end. This is not a forgiving place; even your exit gets a rough going over. And he'd seen several people go down. Said he knew a guy who was killed when a jumper from the fifth tier landed on him, flattening him like a pancake. The jumper lived, at least until he could set himself on fire in his cell, which finally did him in. The other guy, the pancake, was heading to chow and never knew what hit him. That was prison. A certain arbitrariness, violent and quick, was a part of the landscape, like asphalt and weeds. Didn't I get that?

"Mister, ah, mister... I didn't get your name. I'm having trouble hearing you. What gives? What went down tonight?"

He looked at me with that air that he was the adult, me the child, and slowly extracted a razor blade from his mouth. I noticed it was a safety blade, the business end facing out; he'd clenched it tightly in his mouth, hence the gritted speech.

"LaSmith. People call me Smiddy. Motherfucking crazy in this place, my man. Got to be ready."

"With a razor? Mister LaSmith. Or Smiddy.

"Smiddy. Fuck yes. Good as a shank, maybe better."

"Don't the guards pick up on this?"

"Man, it's not like we talk to the hacks in here. Or even to each other, much."

This seemed self-evident to Smiddy, and I had the feeling he'd have said "duh!" if he were one of my sons. But he continued anyway, not something one's sons will always do when you have a little trouble navigating their world.

"They give the orders, I keep my head down, keep moving. I just got to be ready. Plus a lot of guys do this. We don't talk much. Just watch."

"Ready for the sort of violence that jumped off in there?"

"Don't know shit about tonight. Just know shit happens. And I'm ready."

"So what can you tell me?"

"Already did. I'm ready. Shit happens and I go for my blade." After a pause, again looking at me like I'm the child in this deal – "Learned it from a girl. On the street."

On that sobering note I thanked Mister LaSmith for his time. I wondered, just for a second, whether some girl had taught Jones, the Charon Express killer, to swallow razors. Sick thought, but who knew about this razor business who wasn't already living in a sick world?

Smiddy put the blade back in his mouth, nodded, and left. No attempt to swallow. He kept the piece clenched between his teeth. I thought about busting him, but one thing was clear tonight, and that was the cons in that gym were on their own. I wasn't about to play cop.

Donzell King sat down next, gently caressing his hair. Like Ross, he had his hair done that evening some time before the killing. "I had a cut, then a wash out," he announced as he settled himself. I wasn't up on the details of the hair care world but I did wonder if perhaps Jamal had cut his hair.

"Who cut your hair? Jamal?"

"Oh, no. I get my hair done by Pony Man."

"Pony Man?"

"Yeah, I don't know his real name. But he's always shaking his head and he's got this long ma..."

"I get it," I said, raising my hand to stop him. I'd didn't need to know about the details of Pony Man's mane. Prison holds a world full of people with oddities, including a few tics and occasional barnyard fantasies, most of them irrelevant to my work.

I asked, "Did you know the victim?" No one yet had said they knew Jamal other than to point him out.

"Oh yes, I did know Jamal. We was in the chess club together."

I nodded like this was ordinary news, but I didn't even know there was a chess club in the prison. These days the place seemed like a human warehouse and nothing more. Nothing good happened unless the cons pretty much did it for themselves. Hell, the only literacy program was run by a gray-haired volunteer, retired from teaching kindergarten, who recruited prisoners to tutor other prisoners. Nothing sadder than a man facing big time – and likely to die in the joint – who can't read *The Cat in the Hat* without a whole lot of help from another cat marooned here as well.

"Can you tell me something about him, about maybe why this went down?"

"Well all I know is rumors, honey, but Daunte, you know, Mister McFadden, him and Jamal was tight once."

"Tight?" I felt a lead here. In prison, it seems everything is personal in one way or another.

"Oh yes, not tight in a love way, honey. No romance. Neither of them was, you know, looking for love, but they did do some drug deals."

He stretched 'drugs deals' out real show: druuuug dealsss. Meaning serious drug deals, I took it.

I nodded

"Daunte was the small man, you know, and Jamal the big supplier. But they got on, that's what I'd heard."

"So what do you suppose went wrong?"

"Well people in the barber shop do talk, and I can tell you this, word is that Daunte fell behind in his payments."

"So Daunte kills Jamal?"

"Hold on now, Detective. You are Detective Miller, right?"

"Right."

"Let me tell the story. Daunte don't pay but then Jamal has to collect. Word was that Jamal put out a contract on Daunte. Now you know what that means. Daunte don't pay, he gets hit."

"I understand that, but it's Jamal that got hit in the gym and it's Jamal now cooling in the morgue, not Daunte."

"Ain't that interesting? Guess the tables got turned. You know you can make a plan, but it don't make it a permanent thing."

Permanent thing. I wondered if this was some sort of hair dressing metaphor, in which case I was out of my depth. My hair is straight and thinning. No permanents for this detective.

"Can you tell me anything more? Did you talk to Jamal or Daunte tonight?"

"Well no one talked to Daunte. He was like fuckin' Caesar taking over the gym – he came, he saw, he conquered."

"Nobody talked to him?"

"Not that I saw, honey. He came in, sat down, got up to go to the john – at least, that's where he was headed – and next thing you know he's all over Jamal."

"Did Jamal do anything or did Daunte just take him out?"

"I didn't' see Jamal do anything, but he was upset, I know that much."

"Upset? You saw this?"

"Oh yes, just before this went down, I heard Jamal talking about legal work, and he was mad."

"Jamal was talking about legal work before he got taken out?"

"Heard it clear as day. Said to this dude, 'Shit man, you need to get on my case.'"

"Is that all you heard?"

"Well, the gym is noisy so I didn't hear everything."

"Anything else?"

"Well, something about 'a higher court.'"

"A higher court?"

"Court of appeals, I suppose, don't you? Everybody here has something in appeals court. No way out of here except through the appeals court."

Or the morgue, I thought. Maybe the hit man was a kind of court of last appeal. I pursued Donzell on this hit business, alleged hit business, I reminded myself. He'd heard about the hit supposedly going down; claimed everybody had. But nothing specific.

"Can you identify the man Jamal talked to about his case?"

"I seen him around but I don't know him by name?"

"Could you pick him out of a lineup?"

"And then pick out my coffin? No thanks, honey." He waved as he turned to leave. "I've said enough."

The last prisoner, John Gibb, slipped up on me while I was distracted, thinking about what Donzell had said and perhaps a bit irritated about all this "honey" business. I was already calling him 'honey man' in my notes. No matter how many times I hear it, terms of endearment from heavily tattooed men strike me as odd, if not downright bizarre. I guess I lead a sheltered life for a hard-boiled detective.

Gibb was even more decorated than Donzell. A quick and dirty calculation told me the man in front of me was a walking palette of rule violations, some serious, or at least seriously obvious. He was what used to be called 'an illustrated man," an oddity in parts of the world but a common bird in the pen. Still, his plumage, if I can push this metaphor a bit, was particularly impressive.

There were teardrops running down from his left eye, dark black against his light brown skin, announcing to anyone who cared to know that he was a brother who'd never cry again. There was a cross on each ear lobe, and "love" and "hate" imprinted on his left- and right-hand knuckles, respectively. His chest was a playground for a colorful array of dragons and flying serpents, a motorcycle with a helmeted driver sporting a beard down to his waist, and assorted knives and weapons, including a few automatic weapons I couldn't identify. I saw the number 8 above a couple copulating with abandon, his belly button used to strategic advantage, which told me he loved his heroin, even if it had fucked him over in the end.

There was one tat I couldn't quite get, a serpent coiled around a rod or sword, couldn't tell which, a little like a caduceus but I didn't figure this guy for a doctor. Or a magician. I'd learned in one class on gang tats that the caduceus was the magic wand of

Hermes, adapted by some pagan groups as a calling card. But this wasn't a pagan deal, those I'd seen. Fast hands, was that it?

"See anything you like?"

The question caught me off guard. "I'm asking the questions," I replied. I'd been staring at the menagerie that was his body. Maybe I was getting tired.

"Then ask."

"Then sit the fuck still and I'll tell you when to talk."

Gibb settled down quick, seemed almost tame after the opening exchange, at least compared to Donzell, 'honey man' to me, who was unusually talkative for a convict at a crime scene. Gibbs sat down as soon as 'honey man' had vacated his seat but I hadn't seen him in line or seen him at all until he was right in front to me, tattoos prominently on display, standing out like a billboard on a deserted road. It was a little unnerving. I was intrigued, for sure. The man had my attention.

"I'm John J. Gibb. Sorry I gave you shit. Old habit."

"No problem. Occupational hazard."

"My friends call me a lot of things. You can call me John. Or Mister Gibb."

Stripped down to his noticeably faded skivvies and here another prisoner was talking to me like we're sitting together in the park. You had to give them credit.

"Mister Gibb," I said, speaking with a professional tone, meant to convey respect, to let him know I'd taken his lip in stride and wanted to move on, "tell me what you saw."

"I saw whatever everybody saw, and then some. But I aint' talking here. Too public."

"Everybody's stuck here, Mister Gibb. It's not like we can take a stroll down the tier and chit chat."

"Fuck you, Miller."

"Gibb..."

"Sorry, sorry."

"Old habits?"

"Mister Miller, I'm gonna jump up, make a scene – you get me off to hole. We can talk there."

I went along with this ruse because this was a man who had something to say and saying it in private was one of the ways things happen in prison. Segregation – what most folks in prison call the hole – was one of the few places one can have a real talk, though now I'm thinking interrogation, not just conversation.

"So talk," I tell him, once he's safely secured in a segregation cell, after putting up a pretty convincing effort to call me every name in the book and throw a few ineffectual punches in my general direction. 'Faggot punches,' in the harsh, homophobic world of the prison. But he covered well. He had me thinking I was set up and going down hard, and how embarrassing would that be in the middle of a fucking investigation.

"You're a good observer, I take it," I said, to get things rolling again. "Talk to me."

"You can take it that I had Daunte's back."

That sounded promising. "You had Daunte's back? You know him well enough to take his back?"

"We're tight. I'm in the gym watching the game and in come Daunte, a little late, and I know this ain't his game night. I know there's a hit on my man, and I know the hit was put out by Jamal."

"You know all this?"

"Everybody know all this."

"OK, so you figure Daunte is walking into a trap."

"I know he's walking into a trap."

I resist the urge to ask how Mister Gibb knows this; I expect he'll say he knows because he knows or, better, because everybody knows.

"Uh, huh," I say. "What kind of trap."

"A deadly trap, man. He is in a public place. There are no guards to speak of and the gym is a madhouse. It's hot as hell as tempers are short, man. Anybody could slip up behind him and take him out, just like that."

"Come from behind?"

"Or from the side, or from the fucking ceiling. He's out there, man, on a limb. This is Jamal's home. Jamal run the barbershop; Jamal deal the drugs here. People know him and like him."

"Like him?"

"Well, they fear him, and that's better."

"Better in prison."

"Better in any place I've known."

I can't argue that. I figure Mister Gibb has come up hard, and prison is just the end of a trail of bleak places he's called home.

"So Daunte's walking into a jam," he continued, "he's here and he got nowhere to go. So I start to move toward him and then, boom, he and Jamal are into it."

"Just like that? How'd it jump off?"

"I couldn't see real clear. And man, I was shocked. I figured Daunte for trouble the minute he walked into the gym and now, boom, he's got this giant motherfucker down – Jamal is big, man, real big, and little ole Daunte is cutting him up like a Chicken McNuggett."

"Did Daunte just go for him or what?"

"I couldn't see real good, like I said, man, but it looked like Jamal might have made a move toward Daunte, you know, turned toward him, like he was going to say something to Daunte, chew on him a bit. Or do something. But Daunte got the jump on Jamal, that's for damn sure."

"Self-defense, do you think?"

"Well yeah. Jamal want Daunte dead; Jamal meet Daunte where he ain't supposed to be, and that place is Jamal's turf; Jamal come up, not looking like he's there to say 'Yo, Brother, What's happening?'"

I thanked Mister Gibb for his help, told him I'd check back with him later, after I'd followed up on a few things. Gibb had given me enough to get started, I thought, as I picked up my notebook and told Officer James I was ready to move on.

"You done so quick?" he asked.

"Short work," I said. "That jumpy sonofabitch, Gibb, wanted to talk about the game, for Christ's sake. Guy didn't know shit about the killing."

I left it like that. I didn't want word to get out that Gibb had talked. In prison, you play your cards close to the vest.

"I've heard enough for now," I told Officer James. "I'll let the regular officers take the rest of the statements. I've got a few leads and I'm going to ride them down. I want to hit Daunte's house. If he planned this, there might be some clues."

DAUNTE'S INFERNO, PART I

I was mesmerized by the play of light and shadow. The long, sheer line of string cut a graceful arc above my head. Gently guiding its payload – a tightly folded note – the line descended ever so gently to the gray steel floor and then slid under the door of cell 43, not far from where I was standing.

"Remarkable," I said to my guide, Officer Tamika Moore. She'd taken over for Officer James, who had stayed on at the gym. I was glad to walk with her, since she'd been in the gym at the time of the crime and in fact had been the one to get Daunte to drop his weapon on her formidable command.

"The trick is in the wrist," she said, "the flick of the wrist. I busted one guy – they're not supposed to fish – so he told me the mechanics and I let it slide."

"You like to fish? I mean, in the world?"

"No, but I like to know how my world works."

Not a bad idea, I thought. No question this woman was direct and to the point.

"So how do they do that?" I asked.

"You take a long line of thread, like sewing thread, braid it a few times, then throw it out like a lasso, then whip-saw your wrist right, then left, then right, releasing at the last moment. The line sails in the air like it's alive, like it has wings."

"Wings. A valued commodity in prison."

"You got that right, Mister Miller."

"It's like fly fishing. And that, Officer, is an art."

"And you're an artist, I take it."

"I'm a wannabe. I can't fish for shit but guys who can fly

59

fish, geez, it's something to see. A lot of good fishing happens at dusk. The fading light makes the line shimmer as the hook and bait ease their way to the target, drifting like a feather in the breeze, finally landing, silently, slipping through the water and into the waiting mouth of a big-ass bass."

"Seems to me you'd miss as many fish as you catch."

"You'd think so, Officer, but the shadows on the water cast by the line hypnotizes the fish. They follow that hook with open mouths."

"A little like you a minute ago, Mister Miller. Just captured by what you saw. Mouth open and everything!"

I felt myself blush. "That was an amazing sight. Can we retrieve that note?"

"It's gone by now, read and flushed."

"So all this is..."

"Boys passing notes, Mister Miller, like in school. It's like their text messaging each other, like my teen age daughters."

I reflected on this. It was not the first time I'd marveled at the ability of men in cages to communicate with one another, sometimes sharing information, other times sharing drugs.

"So notes are passed all the time, Officer?"

"Oh yeah, constantly."

"From cell to cell?"

"Absolutely. From cell to cell and from different tiers in the same cell block. It takes a little more skill to fish up or down the tiers in a cell block, but folk do it."

"I'm thinking there may be some notes – or clues, anyway – in Daunte's cell, assuming we can find them."

"What you want is a first class shakedown, Miller. A lot shows up, more than you'd think."

"When's the last time these cells been shaken down, Officer?"

"Oh, months, months. We'd have a few 'fakedowns,' but not enough staff to do the real thing."

"Fakedowns?"

"Yeah, you go in, toss a few things around, move on to the next cell. Don't do much damage but it keeps the cons on their toes."

"I like that. We had some fakedowns in the street, easy on the clock, get a man home early."

"Same deal here. Works for women, too."

"Yeah, I can imagine."

"You look too close, you be here a whole shift and more sifting through the weapons and drugs and just plain excess stuff."

"You do the shakedowns yourself?"

"No, not any more."

"Call in a team?"

"Yeah, the specialists. Kinda like a SWAT team but they just search. Guys train for the job, learn about hiding places, practice technique."

I said, "Women trained too, I'm guessing." Couldn't resist.

"Yeah, women, too."

"They practice technique, huh.? I thought they just tore the place apart. Search and Destroy. Isn't that what the cons call them?"

Moore laughed. "They do make a mess, they surely do. And they piss people off. But the officers tell me there's technique, that it's a skill thing. You know, they don't just go crazy. Guy said, 'There's method to the madness.' Told me he heard that in training."

"I don't doubt the madness, Officer. Or that they get folk plenty mad."

Prisons were never accommodating places but these days they can be just plain mean. As far as I've seen, the so-called Search Teams storm the cells like they're hitting enemy bunkers. Throw stuff around and walk all over it; pull stuff apart; take contraband left and right. Tear up postcards and pictures, looking for drugs spread on the paper or worked into it, maybe covered by a layer of wax. In prison, a man can't rightly have much. Most of what he's got is contraband, shit that's not allowed. Sometimes contraband's all he's got. You take that, you pay a price. Or the next CO pays it for you. I'd seen officers attacked after the search guys rolled out. So you don't go home early after they do their thing. Sometimes you don't go home at all. I was glad I was escorted by this officer and not one of the search crew. Daunte'd see them coming and clam right up.

"Daunte's on the top tier, Officer?"

"Check. Cell 509. He's locked down. We got a man outside the door, watching him close, making sure he don't destroy anything you might want to see. Or talk to his neighbors."

"Is this SOP? I'd have thought..."

"Yeah, yeah. I know. Normally we'd have run his ass down to seg. But by the time we got him settled down, the unit was full up and we wanted to keep him away from witnesses, people he might try to, you know, tell his story. Besides, we figured you'd have an easier time talking to him in his house."

"Fair enough," I said. "Maybe he'll feel at home, let his guard down."

No sense telling the officer I'd prefer seeing Daunte in a strip cell, deep in the segregation unit, the proverbial hole, where he'd be disoriented, looking for a way to get out from under all that weight and me working that angle to get some talk. She was just doing her job, and I figured I'd just better get on with mine.

As I started up toward Daunte's cell, Officer Moore put a hand on my shoulder. "Oh, almost forgot. Here's something you need to look at." She handed me a letter, addressed to a Mister Moses Kinley.

"What's this?"

"It's a letter from Daunte to his dad. "

"Mister Moses Kinley?"

"Checked his file; that's his dad. Daunte must have written it before he headed down to the gym."

"You took this from his cell?"

"No, the letter came from the night mail pickup."

"He'd put in the mail? Tonight?"

"Some time this evening, right. We just grabbed it before it got out of the building."

"Thanks, thanks a lot. And good work."

I opened the letter, holding it comfortably in front of me, letting my eyes focus. It read, "Dad, I might have to kill a man tonight. I'm sorry, really sorry. I don't see no other way. I don't see nothin' good, but that's just the way it is." It was signed "D". No dear dad; no love, your son. Just straight talk, if not from the heart, from a clear-headed young man heading into a tight situation.

"Anything?"

"Can't say for sure, Officer. It's only but a few lines." Again I kept case-related information close, not sure who I wanted to know what. "But thanks. It might help."

It certainly might help his dad. He'd read that note, I thought. Read it, and he'd know he'd done something right. Daunte was raised in a ghetto that was like a jungle and now he was living in a prison that was another kind of jungle. He knew how to live in the wild and clearly he was a survivor. "My shank makes me King," one prisoner told me. By that reckoning, Daunte was prison royalty. But the thing was, Daunte had enough sense and decency to know that you do what you've got to do to survive, but that don't make it good. "I don't see nothin' good," he'd written to his dad, "but that's just the way it is." Amen. So his dad should get that letter. I wanted to make sure of that.

I folded the letter and tucked it into my sports coat pocket as I ascended the metal stairs to Daunte's fifth floor perch, at the ass end of the uppermost tier in this huge place we called a cell block or cell house but which was, in essence, a human warehouse. The place was like an airplane hangar, with a ceiling that reached to the sky and walls that faded out of sight in the dusty gloom. And noisy. If you paused for a minute, it seemed like the sound would wrap itself around you, work into your head, get up under your skin, dig down deep into your gut. The assault came from every direction. There were industrial fans, loud and insistent, at the end of each tier, and from every cell came the sounds of radios and TVs blaring and echoing and reverberating until the place seemed to shake underfoot, like the whole building was trapped inside a machine revved up to full gear. I could barely hear myself think, but the susurrations of the summer night, faint yet distinct, gave testimony to a hidden chorus of life amid the mechanical din – crickets, cockroaches, katydids, and the flutter of wings of the errant bird, alert for feral cats, who move stealthily, undisputed predators among a colony of prey, one of them, a tabby, moving saucily under foot, as though I were the intruder, this his turf. The new prisons are sterile and quiet, humming along like computers, but the old houses like this one are menageries, human and otherwise, places teeming with noise and life and, all too often, violent death.

And then there were the eyes. I had the odd sense that I was being watched by disembodied eyes, eyes that had a life of their own, floating there in the cell windows, the cells floating in the tiers, the tiers – even the steps below my feet – floating inside the cell block, this world that looked, from the outside, so solid and bare but was, once you moved to its inner cadences, eerie and unsettling, as if you were lost in a dream. The scene unfolding around me brought me back to my first prison tour, part of my training class in the Academy. We'd come back to the class room, then had to read the work of a college student, now an established writer, who'd written about her first visit to a prison. "I looked around and began noticing eyes," she had written, "fragmented faces of all colors, shapes and sizes peering through small windows in the cell doors. I was reminded of a dark forest, the kind you find in a children's book, with eerie owl eyes piercing the night." The instructor had said, "Read this, gentlemen, and see your world with fresh eyes." Tabriz. That was her name. As in cool breeze, though no cool breeze blew through this prison or any other joint I'd ever worked in. But her words were refreshing, original; she was certainly onto something.

The young woman's words had moved me then and they moved me now. And here I was, once again in that dark and unsettling forest. Right now. The subject – or target – of those eyes, eyes that could mesmerize. But like Tabriz, a part of me wondered even more about the cells *without* eyes. "I found myself drawn," Tabriz had written, "not to the cell windows with faces, but rather to the openings that remained clear of curiosity." The eyes I couldn't see, the eyes "clear of curiosity," that could see me and remain unseen. Or simply wait until I approached and then make an appearance, seemingly out of nowhere. Those were the eyes that mattered most. What went on inside the minds of people in cages who don't even bother to look when an outsider enters their orbit? You had to wonder. Mad men? Bad men? Broken men? Tabriz didn't know; I don't know. But one thing I *do* know is that I always pass those cells with caution.

I braced myself and regained my focus. Sometimes it doesn't pay to think too much. Or too long. I stood confident and erect – for the benefit of the eyes around me, seen and unseen – and walked on deliberately, each step echoing faintly against the metal walls and floors and bars. The dim lighting from the long, barred windows that ran along the outer wall of the cell block added a claustrophobic feel to the place, like you were cooped up, as of course the convicts were, but I felt locked up myself, locked up and making my way deeper and deeper into the inner recesses of a forgotten land. The exterior building windows hadn't been cleaned in my lifetime, as far as I could see. The grime splintered the gray light that fought its way to the tiers, each tier holding some fifty cells in a long row trailing off out of sight into the dark corners of the cell block, each tier in turn fenced in by thick wire mesh, cutting grid marks in the muted light. The mesh was put in place to prevent serious trouble. People had jumped to their deaths from the upper tiers; people had been pushed to their deaths from those tiers, too. The wire mesh was thick for safety reasons but it added to the confined quality of the place, hemming people in, fracturing the little natural light that made its way in muddy rivulets to a man's cell, a 6 by 9 cage illuminated in most instances by a sixty watt bulb hanging from the ceiling.

I told the officer on duty outside McFadden's house to crack the cell door, that I'd run things from here. He moved off a few paces, then set himself in place, leaning against a cell door. It was clear he wasn't going far, and that was fine with me. Every now and again an interview went bad and it was good to have the cavalry, or at least a scout, near at hand. One guy took issue with my name. Or our name. We were both named Robert Miller. Trouble was, that Robert Miller was flat-out paranoid and figured I was messing with his head. Ever try to argue with a paranoid guy who thinks you have it in for him? These guys are relentlessly on message: the world is out to get them, and you are a part of that world. No getting past the bottom line. At one point I showed the other Robert Miller my ID. No good. ID's can be faked. He asked if

I was secretly recording our conversation. As it happens, I had a large recorder right on the table. I pointed this out. No good. Was I doing a *secret* recording, maybe using a device hidden under my shirt collar? This guy, and guys like him, leave nothing to chance. Better to call back up and move on.

I stood back from McFadden's cell, taking a minute to catch my breath and compose myself, to remind myself that no matter how strange the prison was, it was normal to Daunte, who as far as I knew had no mental health issues and was simply a creature of this highly specialized world, like dinosaurs were creatures of their peculiar environments. In fact, I later learned that prison *was* home to Daunte, who'd been raised in one institution or another, a sobering thought.

I knocked, waiting for permission to enter. I'd read that the correctional officers in English prisons knocked before entering a man's cell. That sounded pretty classy to me. Plus it shows respect, a big thing in the prison world.

"I'm here," Daunte said from the far end of his cell, shrouded in the shadow of a funky, urine-yellow light that stained the floor and walls of his monastic home, "can't be nowhere else."

"Hard to argue with that," I said. "Mind if I come in? I'm Detective Rob Miller, investigating the homicide."

I said this matter of factly, like it was no big deal, but Daunte was a sight. He stood before me in a rumpled orange jumpsuit, dark in places with the residue of violence, his neck and arms still slick with traces of blood. I thought I saw dried blood crusted along the edges of his forehead, liked he'd wiped his face with bloody hands and couldn't get enough water from the

68

decrepit porcelain sink – or maybe the toilet – to wash himself clean. The cell was steeped in the musky scent of recent death, like a miasma had settled over the place. Here was a man in a desperate situation, but Daunte didn't look desperate so much as he looked spent, like he'd have dropped off to sleep if the world would let him be. If it weren't for the likes of me, I had to think, a man with a lot of questions, a man who'd give him no time to rest.

Daunte paused, then said, "Do it matter?" not without a hint of anger.

I thought for a minute he was going to say, "Investigating the homicide? Which one?" One guy had greeted me with that, which had thrown me off my pace. There'd been several bodies I hadn't known about. I'd wanted to play it cool with that character – say something like, "Hey, this is prison, who's counting?" – but had thought better of it. Like now. I kept a poker face and started talking.

"Well, you don't have to talk to me, but you're gonna have to talk to someone sooner or later so it might as well be me."

Daunte held my gaze and replied, "And you can help?"

"Maybe. I have some juice with the DA. She'll listen to me."

"She don't listen to shit," he said. "She's the one that put me in here in the first place."

Daunte had killed a man to get himself to prison, but from where he sat, his crime was his business and his prison term was the DA's business.

"No point in debating, Daunte, but she's the one who can put you on the gurney. Put a needle in your arm. You flat out killed an unarmed man in public. It don't look good."

Again, with a level gaze, "And you can help?"

"Can't hurt. I can tell your side of the story, but you gotta talk to me. Or her. But she won't talk to you until you're charged, and then it's pretty much too late. That's the way it works. You deal up front. Just that simple. "

"Like I don't know that?"

"I don't know what you know, Mister McFadden, but I do know this: Be straight with me and I'll be straight with you."

Daunte McFadden was not a man with options. I thought he was smart enough to know where he stood, but you couldn't always count on convicts to have good sense. I'd met or heard of more than a few who'd done crimes so impulsive or just plain stupid it was hard to imagine what they were thinking. One guy, in his early twenties, held up the fast food restaurant in which he worked. In fact, he was reporting for work that night and evidently had a change of heart on the way in the door. So there he was, dressed in his store uniform, complete with some sorry ass paper hat, and positioned directly in the line of fire, so to speak, of the surveillance cameras, cameras that had on earlier occasions been used to prove minor delinquencies on his part. When confronted with this damning evidence, he said, "Couldn't have been me; I was out of town that day." He said this with a straight face, the detective on the case told me.

"Alright, alright. Here's the deal, Miller. I wasn't supposed to be there—in the gym—and, man, I didn't have a choice. It was him or me. Self-defense, plain and simple."

"It doesn't look like Jamal Jordan put up much of a fight. I can't see that he started the fight. Nobody..."

"Nobody saw a thing, right? Nobody knows who started it, right?"

"Right. I can't argue with that. But nobody saw a knife on him, Daunte, and that's key. He was unarmed."

"He ain't unarmed cause nobody saw a weapon. It don't mean nothing happened and it don't mean he didn't have a knife."

I nodded. He had a point.

"But it ain't what you see," Daunte continued, "it's what folks say. That's what counts."

I paused for a second, intrigued by this notion that 'it ain't what you see' in this curious world made up of cells with and without eyes. You could also think of those cages as so many mouths, mouths with big, toothy smiles, each tooth running from ceiling to ground; cold steel, cold smile. Teeth that bite, spitting out words that hurt. "What folks say? You mean, like rumors."

"I don't mean 'like rumors,' I mean plain-ass, flat-out, mother-fucking rumors. I got fished one day and the note say, 'Jamal want you dead.'"

"You got that note?"

"Oh, yeah. I framed it. Got it right here... Miller, what do you take me for? It's in the fuckin' sewer."

"Alright, alright. The note said Jamal wants you dead?"

"Clear as day, my man. Jamal want you dead. It don't say how I'm supposed to get dead or who's supposed to get me dead. Or when. But the message is clear, man, clear as day."

"So you know it's a hit out on you, put out by Jamal?"

"I know that what folks say. Dude wrote the note just passing that intelligence on to me. And if he believe it, I got to believe it."

"You've got to believe the rumors?"

"Listen up. Maybe Jamal want to scare me. Maybe he want to take me down and build up his rep. Maybe he farm it out to a hit man. Maybe it's not Jamal but somebody wants to fuck with Jamal so they drop his name, get him in the shit."

"It gets complicated," I conceded. "I can see that. You don't know the facts but you do know the threat is real?"

"Mister Miller. That's your name, right, Robert Miller."

"Right, call me Rob. Anybody calls me Robert, I know I'm in trouble."

"Like we're buddies."

"Like we got to work together, Daunte."

"Alright Rob," Daunte says, laying it on a bit thick but I can see we're getting somewhere, "you got to listen close. If the word is out that I'm a target, then I am a target. Either the word is true and serious bodily harm is about to be set on my ass. Or the word is false but if I don't act – take somebody down – people think I'm lame. Then some *other* motherfucka will take me down 'cause he think I'm an easy score."

"You can't just walk away?"

"Where I'm walking to, mister... uh, Rob. Where is Daunte McFadden gonna find shelter in this cold world?"

I smiled at this. It's July and we are roasting like pigs in a pan – a steel pan with a corrugated floor as hot as an industrial oven. The night is humid, our skin slick. Brackish streams of sweat are pulled by gravity, pooling at our feet and running to the corners of the cell, our bodily fluids seeming almost to hiss as if ready to boil. 'And yet and still,' as my mother used to say, 'prison is colder than a witch's tit.'

"You smile, Rob Miller. I smile too. But I got to smile, then watch my back."

"You're pretty much on your own here?"

"Well, I got my cell buddy; I talk to him, enlist his aid, as you might say."

I looked around and saw only one bunk, cast in lines of shadow from the play of the blanched light along the cell bars, an oddly appealing tableau, a gift from a clear night and a full moon. I take in a few magazines, one called *Tacenda*. I know the old Celtic word, and wonder what Daunte is doing reading about "things better left unsaid." I didn't figure him for discretion or insight, at least in a literary vein. On the bed, below a Playboy Centerfold, there's a thin paperback with the title, *The Prison Librarian*. I can see the artwork on the cover: a picture of a prison gate leading to a corridor, suffused in soft light, the moonlight glinting off the cover in a way that catches my eye. Can't make out who wrote the book, but I see in handwritten block print, across the top: HOPE. Hope. It's got to be hard to come by when you're in a lonely prison cell facing a homicide charge. Religious material, maybe. Something uplifting, anyway.

"I thought you lived alone?" I said, as my gaze moved from the little stack of reading materials to the rest of the cell, a steel cage so empty I was surprised our voices didn't echo from wall to wall. Some guys filled their houses with stuff. I'm struck by the primitive simplicity of Daunte's little world. "Isn't this a one-man house?"

"Used to be two; turned the other bunk into a desk."

"Nice work, Daunte. Bare, but nice. What broke up the family?"

"Yeah, what split the little house on the cell block? Is that the question?"

I nod. He's playing with me but he's talking.

"Well, me and my homey, we had a parting of the ways. Dude drove me a little crazy. That's a story in itself. But he's still my buddy, my back up."

A golden rule in detective work is to follow any lead and, even more, stick close to home. I wanted to know more about the cell buddy. It occurred to me that Daunte and his buddy may have been in this together, which would change everything.

"So he's still your main man?"

"He is. Once a cell buddy, always a cell buddy. That's the code."

"But he's gone."

"Hey, we had some friction. Dude was on the up and up but he was real particular about how he lived. Man started to get on my nerves with his housekeeping."

"Housekeeping?"

Daunte caught me off guard with that. A prison cell may be a man's house but I didn't think that included housekeeping. Daunte set me straight.

"You're sittin' in my house, Miller. John, uh, well, yeah, John – he kept the house up good. Too good, really. Washed the floors, the walls, even the fuckin' ceiling. Picked up stuff, dusted, you name it, he cleaned it. Or fixed it."

" John?" Daunte had paused when he said the name, so I wondered if that was the man's real name. Then again, convicts can be pretty guarded when they talk to authorities like me, sticking to formal names, giving up as little as possible.

Daunt nodded.

"So this John is, uh, fastidious. A neat freak?"

I could tell this John wasn't an artist. The prison is full of junior Picasso's, some quite good. They can get away with that in the old pens like this one. It's not like the walls aren't defaced by time, if nothing else. Guards see it as therapy, know a painter prizes his work, wants to be left alone. And the work, some of it, was remarkable, not that I'm an art critic but I know what I like. Hell, I'd seen cells with walls like murals, entire walls taken up with nature scenes, scenes with fantastic creatures from deep inside someone's deeply troubled head, blue oceans and bluer skies and even one with a window and a ladder attached to it, this last one so real you thought you could climb out and get on with your life in the world. Oh, and a helicopter, the prisoner's dream, hovers over head in more than a few cells. Hope. It's a hard thing to come by and a hard thing to kill, maybe harder to kill than your fellow man.

"Yeah, he's a little crazy about that cleaning shit. And handy. And he's slow and careful about it. Always working on some damn thing."

It occurred to me that this "John" may have been Daunte's boy or his bitch, or simply a whore, bought for the short run, then sold to next bidder. Some prisons had yard sales, with men going to the highest bidder. Of course this was all disguised – it's not like there were homemade signs saying, 'For a sweet piece of ass, come see Billie in Cell Block Three.' But everybody who was anybody knew the game. And the score. Prison has its love stories, sure. It's a lonely place and human beings adapt. For some, prison brings out their feminine side. Really. Complete with make up, and short-shorts, and even dates. No flowers, but maybe a little hootch, offered to lubricate things, like a man on the outs who brings a bottle of wine to go with a dinner he hopes is going somewhere. But for the most part, sex in prison is a rough business with little room for sentiment. One man had said to me, "I loved my boy," which sounded quite moving; until he went on to say, "It wasn't me just fucking him up the ass." Indeed. Any of these possible relations of Daunte and John would add a twist to the story, something I wanted to be mindful of. The question in the back of my mind was, why throw him out over small stuff?

Instead I asked, "This John have a last name?"

"Do you homework, Miller. His name is Gibb. John Gibb."

"Gibb..." I wanted to know more about Gibb, especially now, him being Daunte's cell buddy, but before I can finish my thought, Daunte's back talking, warming up to this topic.

76

"So one day I look up and the dude is working on making a dresser – a dresser with draws, for Christ's sake."

"A dresser? For the cell?" I don't see one so I assume it went south when the living arrangement went south. Alimony? I was getting ahead of myself.

"Yeah, Miller. Made of cigarette wrappers. All colorful and put together like a picture book or something. Camels, Marlboro, and Lucky Strike. Maybe a few others; I didn't look too close. He said he picked them out special, to make the cell look like a home."

Daunte paused, then held my gaze. "That's when I knew I had to kill him."

Daunte flashed a smile I can only call impish, if you can imagine an impish smile on a man who had, only hours earlier, destroyed another human being in a crime that amounted to a bloodbath. But I laughed; I couldn't help myself. He'd played with me and he got me. And the laugh reminded me, if only for a second, that there was a full-blooded human being inside this man, a man who has killed another human being but still a man with warm blood coursing through his veins and suffusing his face when he smiles. This is the sort of thing I don't want to think about. Human beings inside the convicts, convicts inside the cages, bodies of real people inside the prison morgue, perhaps the loneliest place on the planet.

"You might be alright, Miller. Rob." That smile again, full face, a moment of connection.

"You had me going, Daunte. Fucking wonderful. 'I had to kill him...' Or tell him to move on," I said, trying to get the interrogation back on track.

"Absolutely. We stay friends, but keep a little distance."

"And he's OK with that? He got the dresser."

"Yeah he's OK with that. And yeah, he got the fucking dresser. We still close. When the note come, I ran it by him. When the call come to go to the gym tonight, I said to myself, 'My man is in the gym; I'm covered.' This was his night in the gym. I knew he'd be there watching the game."

"And watching your back?"

"Yeah, for sure. I saw him when I walked into the gym, knew he'd be in the gym, knew he'd be there for me."

"OK, just to back up for a minute, you get the word fished to you in your cell. Who sent it?"

"Don't matter."

"Matters to me."

"I don't know for sure, Rob Miller, and anyway I'm not telling. The word comes, like from on high, and I know I got to ready my self."

"Sounds almost biblical, Daunte."

"It's big-screen biblical to me, Miller. This is my life. And I'm on notice that someone wants to end it, situate my ass on a slab."

"And that someone is Jamal."

"Yeah, Jamal."

"The note says that?"

"We been over this, Rob Miller. The note say Jamal. May not be Jamal but I got to figure it is Jamal. It makes sense. I got a problem with Jamal; now I know Jamal got a problem with me. I owed him some money. I stiffed him. Or he think I stiffed him."

"Did you? Stiff him?"

"Yes and no."

"I'd prefer a yes *or* no, Daunte."

"Well, listen up. I owed him some money, then got locked down in seg before I could pay. When I'm locked down, Jamal get bent out of shape."

"Doesn't he get it; in segregation you're off the books. Even the staff know that."

"Right, my man. I'm off the books. But Jamal maybe get some pressure from his homies to show he's tough, so he talk big, like 'I'm gonna get that Daunte when he get back in population.' That shits sound hard."

"And Jamal was a hard man?"

"He's a dealer. All he got is his rep. He slip and everybody walk all over him."

"So you both get it. Why couldn't you guys work it out?"

"Cause I was locked down. And by the time I got out, the hit was on."

"Or the rumor..."

"Right, my man. The deed was in play or the word was out. Either way, there's gonna be trouble. We both know that."

"And you can't just call a truce and talk?"

"He talk to me after he talk so tough, his rep is gone. I talk to him, I look like a bitch. We're gonna get it on, one way or the other."

"No way to get around this? Nothing staff..."

"You see how many hacks on duty at the gym? Two COs, a gym full of prisoners, a bunch of 'em armed, a pretty fair number crazy. All of 'em doing life, if you can call this life. Hey, man, I'm on my own. That's the way it is."

"So why tonight?"

"Cause I got the call to go the gym and I wasn't supposed to be there."

"That's what you said in the gym, right after the killing. 'I wasn't supposed to be here?' Right?"

"Damn right. That's the whole deal. You call me to the gym on a night I'm not supposed to be there and I know something is waiting for me."

"You know? No doubt?"

"No doubt, Rob Miller. There are no accidents in prison."

"No..."

"None. We play for keeps. Nobody makes mistakes. Nobody lives if they make mistakes."

"So you're called to the gym, it's tonight which is not your gym night, and that's all you need to know."

"It's enough. I know something's going down. It could be Jamal. It could be his man, the dude who took the contract..."

"If there actually was a contract," I add.

"It could happen right when I walk in the door or during the game or on the way back to my house."

"But it is tonight. You know that."

"I know that. I believe that. And I was right."

"Well, Daunte. You killed the man. Don't mean he was gonna kill you. I don't have anybody who says he started this."

"Oh, he started this alright. He walked past me, right as we was heading toward the can, and then turned, twisted, twisted like a man doing a baseball swing..."

"He pivoted on you?"

I read about this technique in a book by Jack Abbott, who had made an art form of killing fellow convicts with a rapid pivot after seeming to pass them by, putting them at ease and making them easy targets. At one point we let Abbott get out of the prison but we couldn't get the prison out of Abbott. His first conflict with a civilian – a waiter in a restaurant, over the use of a rest room reserved for staff – led Abbott to knife the man to death, like the man was a convict who'd shown him disrespect, using his pivot move. The waiter never saw it coming – we know this because Abbott acted as his own lawyer and described the scene in frightening detail, even adding that the victim was *lucky* to be murdered by a pro like Abbott, who killed clean and quick, his prey never suspecting a thing. So my thinking was, whatever Jamal was doing in those fateful moments in the gym, and he may have simply been turning to face the approaching figure that was Daunte, seen through the eyes of a prisoner, his movements could look damn threatening.

"Pivot. Exactly, Miller. He took a step across my path, just a foot ahead of me, then turned sharp – pivoted. I know a knife is coming next."

"But the only knife they found was yours?"

"Rob, this is prison. Knives everywhere. Knives nowhere. You got sorry ass knives no bigger than a limp dick and swords that make a grown woman cry. All kinda knives, man. His knife could be in a sewer half the way to the city."

"You actually see a knife?"

I asked, even though I knew the answer. He couldn't wait long enough to see it, and one way or the other a knife materialized in his mind's eye. The house was full of knives, big and small, like he'd just said, so the smart money was always on a knife in the picture.

"Do it matter? It was there. I could feel it."

"So you just walk down to the gym, set yourself, and then get the jump on him?"

"Well, it sound that way after it's a done deal, but it was an ordeal, man, an ordeal from the minute the word come for me to report to the gym."

DAUNTE'S INFERNO, PART II

I wasn't sure I was ready for an ordeal but I didn't see any choice in the matter. And in one sense the notion that the killing had been an ordeal was refreshing.

Many people in prison talked about killings with a cold-blooded detachment. One guy – a little crazy, but that's pretty common on this beat – talked about killing as if it were a matter of physics, "things happen in the universe" sort of thing. I tried to go with the flow, like this was a normal way of thinking. That people just turned up dead now and again. No big deal. His eyes said as much. No big deal. Shit happens; murder happens; bodies pile up. Big, black, baleful dead eyes. Shark eyes. I'd always thought it was a joke, the idea that some guys had dead eyes, like shark eyes. With this guy, I wasn't laughing. He fixed me in his dead-eye stare and I knew this was a different kind of cat. Crazy, but more than that, dead inside.

I'd asked him, the man with the haunting, dead eyes, "Would you tell me how this happened? How the man, uh, died?"

Now I knew the man was murdered but saying he died was less direct and confrontational. It was also oddly understated, and I wanted to move slowly, deliberately, in tune with the methodical, detached demeanor of the suspect. Suspect! Another helpful evasion. The vic was killed during a lockdown, in their shared cell, so it wasn't a mystery who killed the man's cell mate. Excuse me, cell buddy, just as John Gibb was Daunte's cell buddy. Or former cell buddy. My murderer calmly told me that's the term, cell buddy. Another term for cell mate is bunky, which seems even more bizarrely intimate than cell buddy, for my money. Who killed your bunky? Is he dead because he was funky? More than a few men got killed 'cause they didn't bathe enough. Smelled funky. Or maybe a sexual thing – killed because he was hunky? Made that last dance 'cause he couldn't keep it in his... Even to ponder these questions was absurd. Made me think of Mister Rogers wandering into this godforsaken neighborhood, complete with Cell Buddies, Bunkies, and Cookies for the Killers.

The guy had me rattled, which was why my mind was jumping around, seeking a little escape in humor. But there was nowhere for me to go but to the case, the details of the case.

I knew this man's cell buddy was not a good buddy. He'd been killed with great violence in their two-man cell, behind a locked door, but I was being indirect here, like I said; I didn't want to spook this guy, who looked jumpy to me, ready to call for a lawyer at any minute. I live for confessions. Makes my job easier, helps the courts, too. Pretty much a matter of working a plea deal, no ordeal in the courts that way.

"I just snapped, just lost it," he'd said, first words out of his mouth, his eyes blank, his tone flat, his face devoid of animation, then and for the entire interrogation and maybe for every sorry day of his life, for all I knew.

"You just lost it?"

"Yeah."

"And how did that happen. How did you snap?"

"How did he get killed? I don't know. It just happened."

"OK, you don't know how he got killed?"

"I don't know. I can't explain it. It just happened."

"Were you mad at him?"

"At times. At times. Off and on."

"Where you mad at him when you snapped?"

"Really angry? Killing angry? No."

"You weren't killing angry but the man was killed. Your cell mate."

"My cell buddy."

"Your cell buddy."

"That's what he's called: cell buddy."

"Right. So what happened?"

"He brought this on his own self."

"I see. How did he do that?"

"By being stupid. A stupid bitch-ass pain in the ass."

"What did he do?"

"He sang."

"He sang?"

"Yeah, he sang. Listen up."

"He sang to you?"

"Sang *at* me, man. Not to me. Who the fuck sings *to* other convicts? Good way to get dead."

"Sorry, I see your point." I also thought the man in question was good and dead anyway, even if he had the sense not to sing to his cell buddy.

"Alright."

"So he was what, rapping at you?"

"Yeah."

"And that pissed you off?"

"It didn't bug me at first, but then he started talking in the cell and telling me he wasn't talking to me, just talking to the walls."

"What sorts of things would he say? To the walls."

"You know, like he was gonna rob me, kill me, leave my body in a heap in the corner of the cell."

"Sounds pretty threatening to me."

"He started talking on the tier, making me look bad. And then he wrote some sort of letter to one of his homies, saying he was gonna shank me."

"So he was out to get you?"

"He'd been on me, and then he'd say, 'why are you crying on your bunk, man?' and 'who the fuck are you talking to all the time?'"

"This upset you?" I was beginning to see this as a mental case. Not so much psychopath as pure psycho.

"Yeah, man. It's hard. I try to act normal, you know, but I'm hearing voices. It scares me."

"His voice?"

"No, man, voices. More than one voice. A whole fucking rap group full of voices. Scary fucking voices."

"And he asked, 'why were you crying?'"

"I was crying because I was scared. And then he tells me he's hearing voices, too."

"He was hearing voices too?"

"He was fucking with me. Thinks it's a big joke. Pissed me off."

"Enough to kill him."

"Enough to tell him to leave me alone if he want to stay alive."

"Did he listen?"

"He dead, ain't he?"

"How did he, uh, get dead?" This is where we'd started, but I was making progress.

"He was found dead on the floor, the cell floor."

"How did he get there, on the cell floor. Dead. Is it because you kicked him and he fell to the floor." I knew from the file the victim had been kicked.

"He was on the floor when I kicked him."

"Did you hit him with something and knock him to the floor?"

"No, he fell."

"He just fell? Standing one minute, next minute on the floor?"

"He fell because I choked the life out of him, killed his sorry ass. Choked him and dumped him on the floor."

"I see. Was he dead when you, uh, placed him on the cell floor?"

"Listen up. I didn't place him; I dumped his sorry ass like so much trash. Motherfucker was nothing but trash, garbage."

"And nobody heard anything? Nobody called out to the CO?"

"No. Nothing like that. Surprised me, really."

"Why?"

"Figured somebody would hear. 'Cause his head made a loud noise when it hit the floor. Thump. Dead weight, you know?"

"Dead weight?"

"Dead weight."

"Was he dead when he hit the floor? When you dumped him and heard his head make a loud thumping noise when it hit the floor?"

"No. I thought he was. Sounded like he was."

I was thinking the same thing, so I nodded my head in agreement.

"You know, like his head was a, a chunk of concrete. But then he moved. So..."

"So you did what?"

"Stomped on his head. His neck, really. Figured I'd break his neck, let the fucker die slow."

"Did he die slow?"

"Not slow enough. Started whimpering and shit. What a bitch! So I cut him, cut his throat. Then he died slow."

"What did you cut him with?"

"A razor. My razor."

"Where did you get the razor?"

"It was just a regular prison razor, part of a plastic deal. No big weapon, but sharp enough..."

"So you broke the plastic shaver and used the blade on him?"

"Plastic was already broke."

"You broke the razor earlier, to be ready."

"No, man, we used the razor to cut pictures out of magazines. You know, like he would pick out a hairdo he'd like. I did his hair sometimes."

"With the razor?"

"Yeah, with the razor. And I cut out dogs, big dogs. Out of magazines."

"Was this like a hobby?"

"Cars, too. I'd cut out cool cars and make believe I was riding around in 'em. Outside. Riding out in the world."

"Out in the world?"

"Just something to do. It's not like I'm crazy or nothin'. Not much to do in the cell."

"And you needed a razor?"

"To kill his ass? No, I needed it to cut out the stuff, cars and stuff, from the magazines."

"I see."

"And to cut his hair, man."

"Right."

"They don't give us scissors, you know. Too dangerous."

"Too dangerous. Scissors?"

"Yeah, man. But we got to shave, and this little blade, well, it work good enough."

"Good enough to kill a man."

"Good enough to shave, mostly. Good enough to kill a man if he out stone cold on the floor. Wouldn't want to go to battle with this shrimp dick shiv?"

"Shiv, yeah."

"A punk weapon. A real weapon is a shank."

"I can hear the difference, yeah."

"You can feel the difference, that for fuck's sure."

"So you choked him and got him to the floor. What were you thinking?"

"I wasn't thinking. I was listening."

"Listening?"

"Listening to the voices. Ain't you listening to me? They said, 'kill this bitch. He know you ain't shit.'"

"Voices said, 'he know you ain't shit?'"

"'He know.' That's what they said. 'He know; he got to go.' Bad enough that I know. And he telling his homies so everybody know."

"So he had to go."

"He got to go, and now he gone."

"One last thing. Why did we find a rope around the man's neck?" More intel from the file.

"Sound like overkill to you?"

"Overkill?"

"Yeah. Overkill. Like overdrive."

"Uh, yeah, something like that." I'd never thought of overkill in such a literal way, so it seemed odd. Then again, the whole interrogation seemed odd.

"Before I cut him, I tried to strangle him, hang him. But the shirt – I tore up his shirt, used that – keep slipping. So I said, fuck it. I'll just cut him."

"I see."

"So he bleeded real slow. I guess cause of the noose, you know the shirt, tied around his neck."

"I guess so. Slow."

"Real slow. That's the way I wanted him to go, so it was OK by me."

"OK by you?"

"Yeah. I got time, man, nothing but time."

Daunte had plenty of time on his hands, too, but his story was more complicated than I'd anticipated and I wanted to get to the bottom of it while Jamal Jordan's body was still warm. I sat back, held Daunte's gaze, and forged on, ready to hear about his ordeal.

"Alright, Daunte. Break it down for me. If I'm gonna help you, I gotta put myself in your shoes."

"My shoes, man! That's the key, the real deal."

He smiled. I looked but I didn't smile.

"Alright, my man. I get the word and I get my tool, my shank. You know from shanks, right?"

"Daunte," I say, "I work here, remember?"

"Thought you might call them shivs. Lots of staff call them shivs. No such thing as a shiv; a shiv is gay. Sound almost French. There's just a shank, a hard-ass home-made knife. A real weapon."

"I got that."

"OK, so I get my shank and I put it in my shoe, nestle it up under the sole, so I can take it with me through all the security..."

"So you were ready. I get that. But let's start at the beginning. How'd you get the word, Daunte? How'd you know to go to the gym?"

"The CO came by and said, 'McFadden. Daunte McFadden, out to the gym. Game time.'"

"So this set off alarms."

"Goddam right. Now I'm a player, right. I play for Armed 'n Dangerous, that's my team. I'm a guard, a shooting guard on A 'n D, I bring the ball up, take it in to the hoop when I can, shoot from the perimeter when it feel right, and pass when it don't. I run the team. But see, we don't play on Tuesdays and this fool CO is telling me to head off to the gym. The hairs on my neck are standing at attention and I just know, man, this ain't right. A civilian might think, 'Hey, this is a clerical fucking error. Run with it, get on down to the gym and watch the games.' Thinkin' like, 'It is tournament week, right, and if you coulda' been there you woulda' been there. So relax, man, go with the flow, check out the game.'"

"But you're not buying."

"I'm not buying. In prison, there ain't no such thing as an accident or mistake. I told you that. Everything here is planned. Even chillin' in the cell's a risky business. Some fool could fire bomb you and keep on moving, and I've seen it and I've smelled it, so don't look at me like I'm bugged out."

"I don't think you're a crazy, Daunte." I'd seen plenty of burned bodies in my time. I knew this was a deadly place. "But hell," I said, "officers make mistakes here every goddamn day. Plenty of 'em. I mean, maybe you're looking too close at things, you know? The CO may have just picked up the wrong list."

"Easy for you to say, Miller, but I don't take nothin' for granted. So I said, 'Yo, CO, I'm ready to go.' Sometimes I rap like that. It's not like I'm so happy I sing, like back on the plantation, it's just a way of talking. So he says, 'Here's your pass, man. Y'all go and kill 'em on the court, my man.'"

"Kill 'em on the court?"

"That's right. I don't miss a beat but hey, 'kill 'em on the court?' Is that a sign or what? Hack thinks I'm playing ball tonight, or he thinks I think he thinks that. 'I'll knock 'em dead,' I say, 'just let me get my shoes on and I'm outta here.'"

"Knock 'em dead?" I'm not sure what to make of the language here.

"Hey, I got a sense of humor. Somebody gonna die tonight, that's how I'm seeing it, just don't want it to be me. Now my shoes are ready, been ready since the rumors started. I slip my foot into the left shoe, ease it in slow, move it around a bit, get the shank positioned just right, like it's some kinda Dr. Scholl's insert. I get it just right, the head of the knife just below my big toe, the blade running along the side of my foot, you know."

"The insole."

"The insole, the handle firm up against my heel. I've packed it in with some cotton in the middle so it bends, kind of, when I walk."

"You fit that weapon in your shoe? And walked all the way to the gym without a limp?"

"I broke the shoe in good. And man, when your life is on the line, a little pain in the foot ain't shit."

"I see your point."

We both smile, a tight smile, and just for a second.

"So listen, Miller, I stand, flex my foot, put it down gentle, then say to the CO, 'I'm outta here' and walk real cool out the door of the my cell and head on down the tier toward the stairwell."

"He stayed there and watched you get your shoes on?"

"Yeah. I didn't think much of it at the time but maybe he was makin' sure I wasn't armed."

"Armed and dangerous," I say, letting Daunte know I was listening.

"So, man, I head out, use a slow pimp roll in my stride to hide the fact that the left shoe is a little rigid – it pinch a bit, man – so I push off slow and long, dragging the left leg behind me so I don't put so much pressure on the shoe, you know, the one with the knife."

"It's in your left shoe."

"Right. I'm kinda used to this shank-in-the-shoe business. There's some nights you need your shank and you don't leave home without it."

"Like your Visa?"

"More like a passport. My credit's not that good."

He smiled, and I said, "And you've got a passport?"

"Fuck you, Miller. I'm making a point."

"I get that."

"This is like a foreign land, where you are armed or you are dead. Your weapon is your passport."

We both thought about that for a second. Then I said, "So you head out. You go straight to the gym?"

"Nowhere else I'm headed, Rob Miller. The gym is like the battlefield and I'm heading into combat. I'm a warrior and I'm going to war. But, you know, I take my time, take in my thoughts, figure this may be, you know, my last walk."

"So you want to go slow."

"Go slow. And think, man. It's not like my life flashed before me but I wanted to, I don't know, take things in. This is serious shit."

"Say goodbye, sort of?" I winced, immediately regretting my choice of words.

"I'm not saying goodbye. Or at least that's not all I'm saying. It may be goodbye but I fully expect to stay alive. That's what I'm hoping, anyways. But, I don't know, I just want to know what's going on around me, I don't want to just rush off to this thing."

"What do you do, stop and visit along the way?"

"No visits, Miller. This ain't no social thing. I'm in no mood to talk. But I'm thinking and wondering, you know, what has my life come to and why, you know, why, why am I walking into what might be a trap..."

"A box canyon."

"A box canyon. A dead end. Exactly. Ain't but one way in and out of that gym."

"So are you laying your plan, playing out your options?"

"No, man, I'm just pondering this fucking place. Is my life going to end in this shithole? Is this what my life's gonna come to? I know it might, man, I'm playing to win but this place is full of losers. I'm thinking as I go down each tier, man, this place heavy on people getting paid back, man, burnt for what they done to others."

"Burnt?"

"Yeah, well, this place is up in flames in some part or other seems like everyday, but I don't mean burnt by fire. I mean burnt by life. Just about everybody in here been treated like shit, then they act like shit. When the shit hits the prison, people just soak in it, stew in their misery, man, like this is one big hot pot cookin' the life out of 'em."

Daunte was getting a little philosophical for my taste, but he was talking and I was listening. I figured he'd get us to the gym in due time.

"Stewing?" I repeated.

"Yeah, stewing, brewing, brooding – about how they got where they got and how they can't get out, can't never get out."

"And you saw this, or thought this, on the way to the gym?"

"Yeah, I mean first place I stopped, stopped and thought about things; first place I passed, you know, was lockdown. Seg. Segregation. That's where the outlaws live. Some of these guys are my peeps but a lot of them turn sour in there."

I thought it was considerate of Daunte to give me the various formal names for seg, like he wanted me to get it straight. And I did. Instead of thanking him, I just followed up on what he was saying.

"Sour?" I asked.

"Cruel, man. They so angry they just want to hurt people. Even themselves, if it come to that."

"That's why they're locked up, right? So they can't hurt people? Or themselves?"

"But when they get out, man, watch out. And when they locked down, they can still do tragic shit."

"Tragic shit?"

"Like torture birds and shit. Cats. Yeah, you think I'm kidding right?"

I nodded. Cruelty to animals hadn't struck me as a feature of our punishment unit. Mostly I thought the men were so lonely they'd treasure the company. That's what I'd seen, in any case.

"Yeah, Miller. These guys, a few of these guys anyways, have gotten hard-ass cruel. They rig up lassos so they can catch pigeons, pigeons that land on the ledge outside the bars, coming for food."

"Food?"

"Yeah, food the guys leave."

"Like a trap."

"Exactly a trap. Then they snare them and pull tight, so the feet come off. No shit. They pull tight and the feet come off. Poor fucking bird hobbled, dead meat now."

"And the men?"

"They laugh. Named one of the birds Stumpy."

"Stumpy! That's harsh, man."

"That's what I'm saying. Stumpy became like the name for all of them, and they were like some sort of sick mascot for the hole."

I paused to consider that. Some teams have the noble eagle; seg had a maimed pigeon. Said a lot, when you thought about it.

"So they become hard," I said, stating the obvious, if for no other reason than to keep things moving along.

"Shit yes. They have become hard, really hard. And I know some of these guys. I knew them on the outs. Prison has fucked them up. Fucked them up worse than their crimes fucked up their victims."

I didn't know what to say, so I just sat there, thinking that we had a nation of convicts doing time in America. Over two million and counting, almost half of them property offenders – small time hoods or low level drug dealers scrabbling and scrambling to get by. People getting out and then lasting but a few months, coming back to the can for missing a meeting with their parole officer or missing a curfew or failing a piss test. How many were getting a worse deal than their victims? And who was gonna pay for this?

"The next floor is Rejection Company," Daunte continued. "That's what that fucking place is all about. Rejection. That's like the name of the game in prison."

I nodded. Men in Protection Company are the prison's rejects; they're the worst of the worst, at least as prisoners see things.

"You got men who raped kids, Miller, come to prison and then some prison daddy rapes them. That's how they get to Rejection Company. You got wife beaters who get made into somebody's bitch."

"Poetic justice?"

"What goes around, I suppose. And then the fat cats, you know, the guys who do stuff like Enron, well, man..."

"Or Wall Street types?" I added, in what I thought was a helpful way.

"Yeah, Wall Street, maybe. Ain't seen none of them yet. But all those rich business cats, they get put on a Jenny Craig and just waste the fuck away."

"A Jenny Craig?"

"Yeah, or a Weight Watchers. We ain't particular. They get their food took; they get to be hungry 'cause they can't even stand up for theirselves."

"So you're thinking, on the way to this battle, that people in prison get what they deserve?"

"They get hurt, that's for sure. And I'm wondering if I'm gonna get hurt, and do I deserve it. You know, I killed a man in the streets."

"I know you killed a man. But that don't mean..."

"I know that don't mean I got to get killed in here. The place'd be half empty if that was right. But my life could end in here, I could be murdered, and I'm thinkin', or maybe just worryin', that this might be how my life ends, and how some folks might think this was right..."

"And this makes you what, apprehensive? Angry? Vigilant?"

"It makes me all that and sad, man. Sad. I got family out there. It makes me sad they might have to bury me so soon..."

I think of the letter Daunte had written to his dad. He'd been thinking about these things, final things, the last rights and wrongs of his life. He hadn't just run off to the gym to do violence and mayhem. He didn't see any options, and to be fair, he didn't have many options. Not real options, anyway.

"So you're ready – ready to fight and maybe die?"

"If it come to that. But I'm not plannin' on dying, like I been sayin'. I'm plannin' on killing my enemy and getting on with my life."

"OK, you make your way to the gym..."

"One more stop, Miller. One more stop. A quick shot."

"A shot?"

"Yeah, a little snort of homebrew. Pruno. Jungle Juice."

"A drink?" This sounded a little crazy to me. Of course, I knew there was alcohol in prison, not to mention drugs.

"Yeah, a drink. No talk. Just a drink."

I wasn't sure what to say so I said nothing.

"Some things you guys know, some you don't," Daunte continued. "You don't know much about pimpin' in the house, not that I'm down with that. Figure you don't care much about that. Not your asses on the line. Just not my thing, anyway. But a few of the brothers run stores, mostly like 7-11's but a few got homemade brew."

"For sale?"

"Well, they don't give it away, Miller. This is America."

"OK, OK. I mean, for sale like at a bar. As in, I'll have a..."

"Miller." Daunte smiles. "Make that a Miller Lite."

"Fuck you, too."

"Alright, Miller. It's just like a bar, but not a nice joint. No place to sit. No music. And no beer. More like bad whiskey in plastic cups, but it does get you a little high, helps you settle down."

"Courage," I said. "The English used to call that courage. Liquid courage."

"Maybe that, too. A little courage. Anyway, man, it's just a cell with a full-on stash – snacks, sandwiches, some blow, a little pruno. A break from this dreary world."

"So you go up to the bar..." This sounds like the beginning of a joke but I'm not laughing. I'm just trying to stay with this story, with Daunte as he descends to the gym, stopping off for a little liquid courage before he walks into a nightmare I can hardly imagine, and I've seen a few nightmares in my time.

"OK, here's how it went down. I hit the flats and I'm just about to go out into the yard..."

"The yard outside the gym, leading to the gym?"

"The yard outside the gym. And my man Mickey... well, his last name don't matter. Not even sure what it is, man. Anyway, my man Mickey, he's a bad ass. You got to be bad to be good at the bar business in prison."

"Deal with holdups, that sort of thing?"

"Yeah, but more like cell invasions. Some scary shit."

I nodded, but this was new territory for me.

"Now nobody messes with the Mick. He hollers to me, 'Yo Daunte!' I walk over. He pours a shot. I drop a bag of chips, slug down the drink. He say, 'another?' I say no. 'It's on the house.' I tell him I gotta go. Then move on. End of story."

I knew about the chips-are-money deal, which always struck me as comical. Hard men hoarding Doritos as cash always seems ludicrous, no other word for it. Blowjob? Six Nachos. A hit? Family-size Kountry Kettle Korn Kernels. "I'll write that letter for three Hostess Cupcakes..." Cigarettes used to be money, and somehow dropping a few Luckies or Marlboros or Camels on the counter to get a little play, well, it seemed manly. Like Humphrey Bogart manly. The real deal. But no more smokes in the joint, so snack foods are king. Chips? Play it again, Sam. And here's a Twinkie for your trouble. Not that I don't get it, and man, these guys take this shit seriously. Things are priced as carefully as the stock exchange, one guy told me, and he wasn't kidding. But I'm just saying, this is a strange part of a strange place.

"So you move on? Don't say a word about what's going down?"

"Not a word. I've got nothing to say. And I don't know what's in play. Does my man Mickey have a part of any of the action going down tonight?"

"Like a bet?"

"Exactly a bet, Miller. People here bet on any damn thing. Hell, even cockroaches races out on the tiers."

I knew this, actually, another little absurdity of prison life. Men tie cockroaches to match boxes and then race them. Winner gets chips, I guess; the loser pays up, one way or another. Gambling is no joke in this place.

"So you think he..."

I don't know, that's the point. I don't think it or not think it. It's just out there. I know this place. So I just move on... 'Night, Mick. See you again. Maybe.'"

"OK, you've got lots of thoughts in your head but now you are there, or almost there..."

"Ground zero."

"Ground zero. What happens then?"

"I walk right on in, female officer pats me down, don't even look at my shoes. Everybody watching the game. I sit down along the baseline, keep my eyes open, just sit there and think, just psych myself up. This might be it; this might be the end for me. And I'm scared but I'm also up, ready. I'm a warrior and I am ready for battle."

"But you're just sitting there?"

"Nowhere to go really, until I figure out what's happening. I'm sitting there figuring trouble will come to me, you know, if it's on. So I slip my knife out of shoe and put it in my lap, cover it with my sweatshirt."

"No one can see it?"

"No way. Dude next to me ask, 'How you doing, man' and I say, 'Just chillin'. He don't see nothing. We watching the game. I'm watching everybody around me. No Jamal. I get up to go the toilet, keep my knife up against my leg, covered by my sweatshirt. And that's when it all goes down. Jamal was on the sideline, maybe hid behind some folks so I didn't see him; and he starts to move to the toilet..."

"Or the barbershop?"

"Don't matter. Either way we cross paths."

"And then he pivots..."

"Right, Miller, exactly. He pivots, I can't see his knife, he can't see mine."

"If he had a knife..."

"He had a knife, Miller. He ain't about to jump me unarmed. No such thing as a prison fight and no weapons. Told you that. So I move fast, hit him in the stomach, he bend down, I grab him by his dreads, pull him to his knees and then I go for the head. I just keep hitting him and hitting him, man, like I'm in a trance. It's like I can see myself killing this man but I don't feel nothing, like I'm watching a movie and I'm the, I don't know, I'm the star. I can see myself killing this man. Then I hear a funny sound, a squish, like I hit jello or something. I see the knife is in his head, man, dead in his head. Right through the eye. Knife stopped there, stuck. And that stops me, stops me cold. I can't believe it. Then it ain't like in the movies. This is raw, man, and there is blood everywhere. Everywhere. On me, on the floor, on him, and the blood is spreading and I'm havin' trouble breathing and I look down and I can see the man's face was gray, like a chalky gray, almost white, Miller, and he sure ain't movin', not at all, and his good eye was flat and dull, like a marble been used too much. He's gone. I'm not no doctor, but anybody with sense could see he was dead and gone; and then boom, the hacks are there and I'm on my knees, praying like, praying that I'm alive, thankful, you know, but praying that none of this is real. But it is real. I'm wet from the blood and I can smell it, smell the blood..."

Daunte wipes sweat from his forehead and takes a deep breath. I do the same. We've both been caught up in his story; he took us both to the gym for a few horrible minutes. I know this scene – the knife plunging into Jamal's eye; Daunte a dark shadow above him, arms pumping, teeth bared – will be played and replayed in the killing fields of my dreams. I'll wake up in Jamal's head, or in Daunte's, or both – the scene unfolding like a horror movie and I'm the reluctant producer. I know, too, that Daunte, this man sitting just across from me, this man sweating like I'm sweating, maybe even a little panicky at the animal violence of which he is capable, is nevertheless someone I am coming to feel something for. Right or wrong, Daunte had his back to the prison wall, a wall that could cry rivers of tears for the men trapped in its unforgiving embrace.

"Now where's your backup, your buddy, during all this?"

"He was behind me. Followed me to the toilet without even a signal; like he knew he had to have my back."

"So you were covered."

"Yeah, knew I'd take the big man down or my buddy would do it for me."

"But you didn't need him..."

"I didn't need him, right. But he had my back. I know that. I owe him. I know that, too."

"Alright, Daunte. I'm gonna have to send you to lockup now. I need to think about what you've told me. You may get to see your old cell buddy, he's down there too. Hole's pretty crowded right now, what with material witnesses and guys with contraband pouring in from the gym."

"Well, you know, the seg cells are bare, Rob Miller. No problem with housecleaning if we hook up."

I wonder for a moment if Daunte wouldn't prefer to lock down with Gibb. Killing is a lonely business, or so I'm told.

"Daunte," I say, speaking softly, "I see where you were coming from. I'll see what I can do."

I mean this, but this is prison, and I figure Daunte's story is both true and false, but true enough to pass for self-defense in the world of Daunte McFadden and Jamal Jordan, two men in a modern wilderness of our own making.

MILLER'S REVENGE

I take a deep breath and try to get a grip. I don't know what time it is; I'm in my office but I'm not sure why I'm there. Or what I'm looking for. I'm standing at my desk, looking at my file cabinets, but they're not quite right. The cabinets. Mine are metal, mundane state issue. These are wood, fine grained, varnished. Craftsman quality. And the labels are different, all wrong. Mine are alphabetical. Simple. Start with A, end with Z. Not these. These have strings of letters in clusters. And when I get closer I see they are names. And numbers.

Last name, first name, number.

I'm thinking, what the... And then I get it. Connors, James 457896; Arroyo, Luis 793362. Clients. Murder vics. These are my clients. Each fucking name is the name of a client, someone I've worked for. I feel a surge of excitement. What a great idea!. Clients. That's what counts, right? Organize the files by client. No other stuff, office stuff, in the way; no policy, no procedure, no office memos neatly tucked away, just clients, by alphabet sure, but just the stuff that counts. Why didn't I think of that before? I browse a bit and come to the one I'm looking for: Jamal Jordan. Or Jordan, Jamal, 174238. I'm thinking Jordan must have a big file. He's the only name on the drawer; he's got the whole drawer to himself.

And then I see that there is only one name on each drawer. One name? A whole shelf for each guy? I mean, we do paperwork and it stacks up, but this is ridiculous. I've got to ask Vittoria about this? Is she putting her files in with mine? Would I mind?

I catch myself drifting off to Vittoria and the possibilities of file mingling on and off the job, and pull my mind back to the file cabinet in front of me, which is still a wonder to me. I figure the Jordan case is closed – Daunte McFadden is the perp, no mystery there, even if I've come to see Daunte as a victim, too. I move toward the drawer, just to check – I'm amazed that this case file fills one whole drawer – but then my eye wanders to the left and I see the words, McFadden, Daunte. And I think, why does Daunte have a file?

Daunte's not my client? He's the guy I've got to bust. I'm gonna cut him some slack, sure, but we're talking a chunk of prison time. He's a perp. He's gonna do big time.

I move closer to Daunte's file drawer. I'm gonna check this out, figure out what the hell is going on here. I pull the drawer and at first it's stuck. I pull harder and it starts to move but it's slow, like the drawer is full of lead. I look inside and I see, well, denim, blotchy red denim, like somebody messed with the files, poured red ink on them. I hear a scream. A long, loud scream. From the next office, but moving toward me. And then it's right behind me. And then it's in my head.

"Rob, Rob, what in the name of the heavens is the matter?" Vittoria was next to me, comforting me, but she was afraid, I could see that.

I was afraid, too.

"The body, Vittoria, what's his body doing in my office?" I knew that sounded crazy even as I said it.

"Body? Here? These are files you are holding, Rob. Rob, please, you must get a hold of yourself."

I started to point but the body was gone. Gone. A file folder fell from my hand, landing at the feet of my metal, scuffed, institutional file cabinet, the one I know, the one with old, worn inserts listing the letters of the alphabet, no names, nothing. And no bodies, apparently.

"Daunte was here, Vittoria. He was. His body was right here. I know that sounds crazy but he was as real as life."

"I know, Rob. I know."

"I'm not crazy, Vittoria."

"I know Rob, but the craziness is in the situation. He is alive one minute, then the next he is gone. What are you to do? Sometimes the human mind – it is an organ, with limits – it can only handle so..."

"But Christ, Vittoria, I saw him. He was right in the fucking drawer..."

Vittoria looked skeptically at my file cabinet, not a likely repository for the body of a man newly killed. She looked at me and I knew I had to get a grip. Got to get back to business.

"Rob, you are in a state of shock. It has been a long day. A day of trauma."

I picked up the file at my feet and vaguely remembered reading it before I drifted into my nightmare. The main thing that had caught my eye was the checklist, a standard institutional catalog of the things prisoners owned. If you could call it ownership. More like leased. Everything was owned by the prison, even the bodies of the prisoners, alive or dead. Or injured. A prisoner who attempted suicide could be written up for destroying state property: his body. Not that the state valued said property very much, but possession is nine-tens of the law, even in this jungle.

Daunte's list was faded and stained and badly dog-eared, long on sundries and clothes, like socks and boxers and sweatshirts, short on anything personal. Everybody, it seemed, had the same boxers, socks, sweatshirts. Something called a "commissary approved roach motel" also showed up on every list of my caseload. I wasn't sure whether the prevalence of roaches or the need for a 'commissary-approved' solution made me sadder. And weren't roach motels essentially prisons – death houses, even – for bugs? Selling approved prisons to prisoners to kill contraband bugs. The irony would be delicious if this wasn't happening every day to millions of people in a zoo near you called your local correctional facility.

All of the men killed in prison had their lives reduced to the items on these institutional checklists. They were individuals, but nothing in these lists spoke of their individual human lives. They were human, of course, but they didn't really live here like human beings. Maybe that was it. More like they just existed here, passing time and hoping time wouldn't pass them by. Meanwhile, they spent their days taking up space in the cells and tiers and yards.

And now, in one day, Jamal Jordan and Daunte McFadden were added to roster of the dead, men whose lives were reduced to these pathetic checklists and whose remains would find their way into a prison graveyard. Or maybe just a plastic urn, more like a jug, really. Unclaimed bodies were cremated, one more fire in this hothouse. Saves space. Nobody wants the remains of the unclaimed, so their ashes are held for a bit, then discretely deposited somewhere outside the prison gate. Free at last, I thought.

Commodities with value, like radios and, for Jamal, a TV, would show up on the checklist but would be nowhere to be found when the man's cell was cleaned out by staff, the good stuff taken by convicts before the vic's body was cool to the touch. Jamal's TV was gone before the officers let the cons out of the gym! How the word got out is a mystery. Hell of a long kite flight, but these guys are motivated. Maybe one of the officers made a call. They'd do it to build a little capital with the cons. Good to have friends on the reservation. Next time trouble goes down, you might feel a little safer knowing you've got an ally in the house. It's an illusion, but safety is an illusion in life, here and out in the world. So you play the hand you've got, maybe cheating a little to get an edge. I don't condone this kind of thing – they called it 'collusion' in the academy, which is a fancy word for working with the enemy – but I understand it.

Daunte had the usual junk that summarizes a convict's life, plus a crumpled letter from his dad. The letter was listed under "other," which shows you how few letters are found in the cells of convicts – not enough to warrant a formal category. Daunte's letter had been found in his right shoe, the one that wasn't used to carry the knife that ended the life of Jamal Jordan. It occurred to me that Daunte didn't want to lose that letter, wasn't taking any chances. If he was walking on it, he must've figured he knew where it was. It was creased badly, and a little smudged. I thought it smelled like sweaty feet but my imagination might have been kicking in. Probably his sweaty feet made the ink run. There was no date on the letter but certainly it was before this disastrous night and well before Daunte's letter to his dad.

The letter was personal, maybe the only personal possession in his entire catalog of things, but in a folksy kind of way, if you can imagine a folksy letter about doing time. Daunte's dad had done time too, judging by the letter. He asked how Daunte was getting by. He'd sent money for commissary. Did Daunte get it? Did Daunte buy those chips he liked so much? He'd arranged for Daunte to get a centerfold for his cell. The writing was smudged here; it looked liked Miss Maple, but I inferred it was Miss May. Inferences are my business I thought to myself, suppressing a smile. Reading on, I saw that dad had gone on to express the hope that Miss May was as good to Daunte as she'd been to him! My smiled deepened before I thought about how depressing it was that a centerfold could be the center of the sexual and maybe even romantic life of two cons, father and son, one dead and one about **to** get the bad news, both shaped in profound ways by the zoo we call prison. It occurred to me, not for the first time, that human animals just don't live well in captivity. Then again Daunte'd had other magazines, serious literary stuff, from what I could tell. So maybe Miss May was just a diversion, something to create a few moments of animal release in this human menagerie. I could understand that. It's not something I wanted to dwell on, but there are lots of things about prison one shouldn't think too hard about if you want to sleep at night.

Of course, Miss May was not on Daunte's inventory, so she was contraband. (Someone could have checked "poster" but hadn't, maybe a concession to Shawshank Redemption, a big favorite in the house.) You could say Miss May never existed. The policy was: "No images of naked women in prison." I suppose it goes without saying that no actual naked women were permitted in prison, but rumor has it that a few of the female CO's were said to violate that rule, though I couldn't find any complaints or write ups on the matter in the main institutional file. The general philosophy was that, a few rogue female officers aside, it was better to let the men go at each other – and especially at the wayward teens sprinkled in courtesy of the drug war, some doing life without — than to subject prisoners to the horrors of pornography. The subject of sexuality in the house depressed me, and I must have drifted off to sleep, perhaps thinking of the savage things we do to one another on a regular day while congratulating ourselves on our roster of PG13 films and Bible readings.

I turned to Vittoria, sobered by my thoughts, wondering if I'd dream about these files tonight and the lives and deaths they catalogued in such spare, cold language. I hoped I'd dream about Jake. And about justice — getting Jake right. That's a dream worth having, maybe the real American Dream. Lock up thy enemy! We invented the goddamn penitentiary, didn't we? We've sure learned to live with it. And live with the killings. I thought about zoos again. I couldn't help but think that zoos were better than prisons in some ways. At least with zoos, people bring their families to visit and have to be told not to feed the captives. Most of us would just as soon see convicts starve, and we sure as hell wouldn't bring our families to see the carnage. We just like to think the cons are animals and leave it at that.

"It's just hard to take it all in," I said, thinking about my reveries and the nightmare that had unfolded in my head and in real time in the prison. "I mean, just minutes, less than an hour after I left Daunte, sent him on his way…"

"There was no way you could have prevented this. There was not a thing you could do," Vittoria said, her soft words softening the hurt, her hand stroking my hand. "Do not torture yourself. There's enough pain to go around; we don't need to be the makers of our own suffering."

"I know, or at least that's what I want to believe. Shit happens in prison. Murder happens in prison. I can't stop it but I hate to think I let one happen. Tonight. Practically right under my nose."

"Under your..."

"It's an expression. Practically right in front of me. Like I might as well have let it happen. Vittoria, I need to see."

We walked together to the morgue. It was unspoken but I needed to see the body, the real body, the one I thought was in my file cabinet, the file cabinet that now seems to me like a chest of funeral drawers, a repository for my worst fears about my life and my work.

This wasn't the first prison dream I'd had. There'd been others, sometimes with me as the victim. Like I was killed for my sins. Or my failures. Letting people get killed on my watch. Or letting the bad guys get away. Or maybe just little mistakes I'd made, and had to die for. Lifers had prison dreams, too. After a while, that's all they dream about: prison. "It's all we know now," one guy had told me. "I can't even imagine a woman. I think about pretty boys in the house." Just calling some of these guys 'pretty boys' struck me as a very, very bad sign. Some of these 'pretty boys' had assholes the size of Texas. But I got his drift. I knew men dreamt about dying in prison, their cells like tombs, assembled convicts in attendance, the affair like some sick wake, all the 'guests' leaving with the dead man's stuff and going back to their houses to wait on their own deaths. And now I was dreaming about prison, and dreaming about dead fucking bodies in my prison office.

At least I wasn't one of those dead bodies, though I hadn't checked every drawer in my dream.

Vittoria and I stood together in the cool, dank air of the morgue, our shoulders almost touching, looking down at the body. The real body of Daunte McFadden. It was, of course, the body of a young black man, and I couldn't help but note that he had been well nourished and apparently healthy, marred in life by a few ragged scars and marked for death by one fresh, bright red wound, neatly traced along his throat, a cut so clean it looked almost clinical.

"Vittoria, I was speaking with Daunte just a few hours ago. He was alive and well. And, sure, he faced homicide charges but he did what he had to do to survive in this godforsaken place."

"Rob, there was no way you could have prevented this. There was not a thing you could do," Vittoria said, her soft words softening the hurt, her hand stroking my hand. "He wanted to live," she said, "and you wanted to help him. You were doing the right thing, yes?"

I said "yes" but I wasn't sure I meant it, or rather believed it. My little dream or hallucination or whatever it was, suggested I had serious doubts on that score. But I wanted to believe her, to trust in her, to get solace from her. "Certainly I tried to do the right thing," I heard myself saying, "but this time I got it all wrong. I'd jumped to conclusions, and Daunte paid for it."

I thought back to my conversation with Daunte. That's what it was, or what it became, not an interrogation. The prison is a Beast, one convict had written, and everybody lived in fear of the

Beast. Sooner or later, everyone fell prey to the Beast. Did Daunte forget this. Did I? Am I a casualty, too, my wounds not yet visible? I wonder, sitting there amiably chatting it up with a killer, starting to like him, even; when I should be interrogating him hard and acutely aware that he might be in jeopardy himself. In prison, the consequences of killings spread out like ripples on a cesspool. I let this shit happen.

"So tell me what happened, Rob. How did he come to our morgue, this Daunte, this man smart enough to live in the face of an unknown hit man in a prison full of murderers and rapists and thieves?"

"Trust, I think, was his downfall. And maybe a little myopia in matters of the heart."

"These are human flaws, Rob. It could be any of us dead in this prison, Rob, if what you say is true."

"Daunte trusted his cell buddy, John J. Gibb, aka Jake, aka Jake the Snake."

"It was his cell buddy..."

"Former cell buddy..."

"...who killed him?"

"Yes, and we served Daunte up on a platter. I ordered him to seg, and when Officer Tamika Moore delivered him, she put Daunte in a cell with Gibb."

"But why?"

"Because the hole was crowded. Because I'd told her Gibb was Daunte's cell buddy and it would be alright. Because Daunte wanted it too, said he could 'kick it' with his buddy and not to worry, we'd talk more tomorrow."

"So this was an accident? The placing of him in, in the way of harm?"

"In harm's way, yes. An accident. Or maybe fate. It was Jake all along. Jamal put out the hit and Jake took it because he was, well, a jilted suitor."

"They were lovers?"

"Not exactly. But Jake thought so – or hoped so. He'd worked hard at the 'domestic angle,' he told me."

"Domestic angle?"

"He thought they were playing house. That's what he said when I talked to him just now, after he killed Daunte." I suppressed a longing look at Vittoria, feeling for a moment some empathy for the unrequited yearnings of Jake the Snake, our cold-blooded hit man. But only for a moment.

"He'd written love letters to Daunte. Love letters, Vittoria. For Christ's sake!"

"And Daunte, he did not admit to this?"

"Daunte never saw them. Or at least Jake never gave them up. 'Too personal,' he said. Maybe Daunte saw them and didn't let on, and maybe that's why he and Jake got up to different living arrangements. But I don't think so. Daunte trusted Jake. He wouldn't trust the man who wrote this letter."

"It is so very bad, this love letter you are holding?"

"You tell me. I see red flags, for sure. Jake called it – he gave the fucking letter a name, like it was a tribute – "Daunte's Allure." It is like a passion thing. It *is* pretty passionate, actually." I said this with a trace of envy, I had to admit. At least Jake had the balls to put his hunger into words. My love life was on life-support and this sonuvabitch is writing love letters!

"A prison love letter? And this makes you uncomfortable?"

"Yeah, it does." Evidently I wasn't as cool about this as I'd thought. "I, I guess because the passion seems real." Felons in love somehow didn't set right with me. But I knew this was wrong, so I added: "Really real, the passion."

"That's good, Rob. When real passion is really real."

I wanted to say, 'No, it's not good' and 'It's not very nice to make fun of a man who is stumbling over his words in delicate matters of the heart,' but I thought I'd quit when I was ahead.

"Just listen to this, Vittoria." I set out to read the letter in a voice marked by longing, which I came by honestly, and maybe Jake did, too: 'He loves me. I am valued in his heart. He cares for my contentment. Revels in my person. Worthwhile for myself. Adored even in obscurity. Hands soft in a rough world. Lovely chest, healthy...'

"Lovely chest? Goodness, Rob. This is what you'd call heady stuff, no?"

It was, but I wanted to say that came later. I caught myself, though. This conversation was already a little dicey, what with me sounding like a bit of cave man with a thing against gay lovers in prison. My humor can get me in trouble if I don't keep a lid on it, so instead I said, "It goes on: 'Lovely chest in a world of starvation. His deep cobalt eyes cannot deny their love for me. Pure liquid of solace and joy. Lips ravenous...'"

"Oh, my." Vittoria blushed, raising her chin a bit, as if to assent to the growing passion in this remarkable letter.

Indeed, I thought. Oh, my. I was liking Jake less and less, and I'd started from zero. I held Vittoria's gaze for a second, then returned to the letter, not unmindful of the fact that if I'd had the sense to keep this letter to myself I might have borrowed a few lines and passed them off as my own.

I plowed on: "Lips ravenous, ready to receive me. Arms envelope me in their protection. People attack me. People ravage me. They will condemn me. They will forget me. But Daunte can have my body. For he will be my friend."

Vittoria said immediately, "His friend? I expected something more, um, intimate. So, when all is done and said..."

I started to correct Vittoria, to tell her it's 'when all is said and done,' and let it go.

"... Daunte was just a friend, Rob? A friend of..."

"I don't think so, at least the way we use that term in the world. I think that a real friend is what Jake wanted, but in prison, about the best you can get is sex. Giving it, receiving it. Words are cheap. Touching, well..."

"The touching, is that what counts?" Vittoria asked.

"People build walls around themselves in here." And not just the cons, I thought. "I see that all the time. Touching means connecting."

"Sort of, if you touch me, I count. If I count, I'm your friend. Your actual friend?"

"Yeah," I said, thinking of the famous line, 'I doubt, therefore I am.' Lots of doubt in the house but nobody finds meaning or solace in that. Just a truckload of self-doubt mixed in with self-hatred.

"It is sad, Rob. Do you not think so?"

I did, but it's not something I like to think about. "And a little desperate," I replied. "Jake yearns for Daunte; Daunte spurns Jake, knowingly or unknowingly. Maybe unknowingly is worse. Like Jake isn't even in the picture. In the end, some twisted notion of friendship, warped by the heat of this human inferno, brings them together tonight, locked in a..."

"Lethal embrace?"

"I was thinking, locked in a cage together. Lethal embrace sounds good, though. It's like a..."

"...snake thing to do," Vittoria added. "And won't Jake follow him. To the same fate?"

"You mean, get himself killed – by someone who wants to front for Daunte or wants to build a rep?"

"Or get himself put to death, in the lethal injection chamber?"

My first thought was that we don't embrace people in the execution chamber, but I can be a bit slow to keep up metaphors, another reason I should've hung on to Jake's letter. After a moment to collect my thoughts, I said: "Ah, the needle. The finale, what some folks call *lethal rejection*, the final intersection in the miles of bad road that lead to prison." I smiled, feeling better. Lethal rejection. Catchy.

"So this will happen? He will be lethally rejected?"

"I doubt it, really. Not like he doesn't deserve it. But we've got dirty hands. We put a killer in a cell with him. Jake will make a self-defense case, I'm sure. It's pretty easy. All Jake's lawyer's got to prove is that Jake had a reasonable fear for his safety, and Jake can make that pretty clear by pointing to what Daunte had done on the gym. Scare any civilian senseless."

"But there are special circumstances that, what, extenuate? Or even point to Jake as a killer?"

"Yes, but it's speculative. Doubt it would stand up in court. A good lawyer would say there is no reliable proof Jake had anything to do with the hit in the gym, and so he was just an innocent victim sitting peacefully in his cell when we, incompetent goons that we are, dropped Daunte into his world like a hand grenade with the pin out. And besides, what jury would care, really, about figuring this all out and making the hard choice to..."

"To lethally embrace or inject or reject him?"

"Exactly. You've got to care enough about the victim to call for the killer's life. That just doesn't happen in prison murders. I've seen this, Vittoria. Juries don't get exercised about prison killings. They loved the details, like the hit man who said he killed folks to keep himself in cigarettes and chips, then added, almost as an afterthought: 'But I didn't do this one. If I'd taken the case, everybody concerned would have been dead and we wouldn't be sitting here.' Thing was, he sounded damn convincing. Still, no lethal rejection for this guy. Just more time."

"This actual hit man said, 'everybody concerned would have been dead?'"

"Yeah, everybody concerned. A great line. But hardly anybody on the jury *was* concerned, and that was the long and short of it."

"So Jake is a Snake. He truly is. His name is a good one for him. He was very, what, slippery in this instance?"

"Smooth, really. Slimy, maybe. And ready to strike when the opportunity presented itself, which it did, thanks to us." I couldn't help returning to this depressing point.

"Just like a snake. Many of them die on the road, yes?"

"Yeah, no question," I said, worried I might be getting out of my depth here. The road of life? I wasn't sure exactly what she meant, so I decided to get back to the basics, getting away from metaphors and getting back to straight up killings in the house that had dominated this very long day. Somehow, stating the basic facts was a comfort. "Jake was deceiving Daunte all along. It was Jake waiting in the gym for Daunte," I continued. "Daunte saw him and felt safe, but it was Jake coming up behind Daunte to take him out, to show the prison world that nobody dumped Jake, that if Jake couldn't have Daunte, nobody could."

"The hit man's actual words again?"

"Yeah, his actual words." I suppress a smile; somehow Vittoria has made my statement comically precise. "'If I can't have him, nobody can.' Trouble was, Daunte took Jamal down fast and Jake backed off."

"So Jake waited for his opportunity. In his hole."

"In *the* hole, Vittoria, not that it much matters now."

"In the hole, coiled—is that right? Like a snake is coiled to attack?"

"As it turns out, just like a snake, that sonuvabitch. He played me, then played Daunte one last time. I talked to him in the gym. He was real cagey, I see that now, looking back. Played me.

Talked his way into the hole and I played right along. Knew Daunte would end up there; wanted to get himself there first, to be ready."

"Could he be so sure he could kill Daunte there, in that hole?"

"Not sure, but it was a good bet. After, he told Officer Moore he'd wait a lifetime, if he had to, to get Daunte. This was one ploy, an early move, and it worked."

"He didn't have to wait long because..."

"...we brought Daunte to him."

"I'm sorry, Rob. This could not have been foreseen by you or any man."

Or woman, I thought. But instead I said, "that's the way it was, really. We brought Daunte right to his killer's cell, for Chrissakes. To his cell! And with smiles all around. 'Jake,' Daunte said, according to Officer Moore, 'my buddy.' If I'd been there, I'd have put it together. I didn't know John was Jake, let alone Jake the Snake. But soon as I'd heard Jake, I'd have put it together..."

"But Officer Moore didn't..."

"Couldn't. She didn't know. Only I knew about this Jake the Snake business. I was keeping that lead to myself; I didn't want the word to get out, put the hit man on notice. That sort of thing."

"That is normal detective work, yes?"

"Yes, but just maybe, Vittoria, just maybe I didn't want anyone else breaking the case. And then I sent Daunte to his death. I was blindsided. Or maybe just blind."

We look down at the body, a body seemingly robust enough to rise from the steel table in search of revenge, to redress this wrong like I planned to redress this wrong.

"How many doors do you figure closed on a guy like Daunte, how many daily insults and losses ran together to bring him to the prison gate."

"A gate he could never open, even if he'd lived."

"And he expected to live. I'm sure of it. His last words, last word, really, was 'Jake?'"

"A question?"

"A question. Like he was surprised. That's in the report; guy next door hear it, told Officer Moore. I'm guessing Daunte figured it out in that last instant. And Jake, well, the sonuvabitch told me point blank: 'Payback is what prison is all about.'"

"And you know, Vittoria," I said after a long pause, "he's right."

"Does this Snake, this man who smiles and kills at one and same time, does he know the truth of this, Rob, this philosophical observation, if that's what it is?"

"Not by half, Vittoria, not by half."

I hadn't corrected Vittoria earlier, when she spoke of the hole. Or I hadn't told the whole story. Most folk around here call the segregation unit the hole. That's what Vittoria meant when she was talking about the hole: segregation, the normal punishment unit. That place is a nightmare in its own right, but only a few of us know there is an actual hole, carved out of rock from the earliest days of the pen.

'"Where he's going is special, Vittoria."

"Special?"

"Well, let's just say it's wet and it's cold, more like a dungeon, which it was..."

"A dungeon. For heaven's sake, Rob. A dungeon! In this prison!"

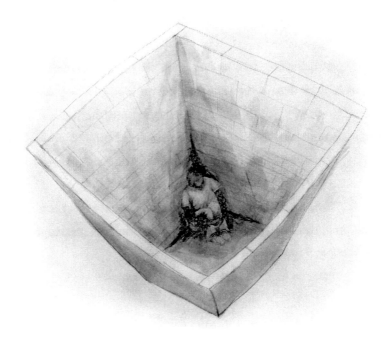

"The guards who escort you there are the classic goons, throwbacks to an earlier prison time, some of them so big they look like giants, so mean they act like criminals."

"I may have seen some of these, these men... I thought they *were* criminals."

"Well, don't rule that out, though they don't have rap sheets."

"Rob, it is like you are speaking in the form of riddles. What is this place called, Rob? It sounds horrible."

"It *is* horrible. It's the *real* hole, Vittoria. Most old joints have them, use them only rarely. I've been there, Vittoria. The first thing that gets you is the musty smell. The air is sharp, pungent. It's hard to breathe. It's like you're drawing in shards of glass when you breathe. I know my heart was beating fast after just a few minutes in there."

"Is it a dirt hole?"

"No, not now. It was at first. Now it's like an underground concrete bunker. The paint is old and chipped; the walls have shifted, maybe from the pressure of the earth, or just from age, and so the place is lopsided, which makes you feel like you might be crushed one day. There's a window but it looks out into dirt, a wall of dirt. The toilet is a hole in the floor. The place smells like a cesspool, which in a way it is. It makes you feel like an animal, so we reserve it for the real animals, animals like Jake."

"In cases of extremity, like this one?"

"Like this one. Jake the Snake's a menace. He'll slither down into the hole and never see the light of day."

"Never?"

"Well, let's just say he'll never be the same, Vittoria. Payback, like the man said, is what prison is all about."

I left work that day feeling like I'd done something, had an impact, made a dent in the violence that sweeps through the prison like a dark wind from below. It was an illusion, of course, but a comforting one.

I don't like to think of myself as a vengeful man but at times the hopelessness all around me in prison makes me burn with resentment, makes me want to lash out. I'd found a poem about prison violence some years back that pretty much said it all for me. I'd asked Vittoria if she'd like to hear it.

"Ah, poetry," she'd said. "I love a good poem. Read it, please, with the feeling of seriousness it deserves."

I nodded, hoping I was up to the task. "It's called 'Eulogy for Sorei,' written by a man named Elmo Chattman."

"Chattman. Don't I know that name?"

"I hope not," was my first comment, since most of the people Vittoria knew were quite dead. "He's a lifer, Locks in Cell House H, last I heard."

"H? Which stands for Hell?"

"No, any of the cell houses could qualify. I think it was just the seventh block opened up back in the day."

"Oh, I see."

"And now listen," I said, gently. "This is good, really good."

EULOGY FOR SOREI

I saw a man die today

-

Actually it was years ago
a MILLION years ago
but his death has never left me
It is etched on my eyeballs
like a lithograph
Now when I see the world
it is always red.

-

"Help me," he cried
Rather, his lips formed the words
There was no sound
Only the silent whisper of death
His hands clutched at a spot just below his throat
trying to stop the fountain of red
spurting from the hole in his chest...
The little boy
with his finger in the dike.

-

The others looked on for a moment
then were gone
turned their backs and hurried away
lest they be the one accused
It was as if the poor man had the plague
In that moment
he did
In that moment
he hadn't a friend in the world.

-

There were jeers and cheers
Since when had death become a spectator sport?
Thumbs up
Thumbs down
Are we Romans?
It really didn't matter
His final curtain was coming down fast
There would be no encore for Sorei tonight.

I stood there torn in two
like a valentine from a confused and forgotten lover
My heart told me to go to him
but my feet stood fast
The convict in me knew better.

-

Sorei died before he was touched by another human hand
His last taste of mankind
was not kind at all
Betrayed by the kiss of the assassin he called his friend
Something inside me felt the blade and died with him
The scars in my eyes
these cataracts of death
prove it.

-

Today it is life as usual in the pen
Broken men wander to and fro
their anger and passion, pent up and stifled
becomes the enemy within
Sometimes I hear them on the yard
boast to the young boys fresh from the world
"I was there when Sorei died
I am a soldier
Don't fuck with me."

-

I look at them through the bloody windshields of my eyes,
wondering what planet they are from.

Vittoria was silent, her lips pursed. "He lay dying, right in the open, untouched. So many people but so alone. And so bloody. Bloody windshields. Such an image. I can see it, really."

"Though not clearly," I said, a weak attempt at humor.

"What, Rob?"

"Nothing. I'm thinking bloody windshields are standard equipment on Planet Prison. That's where the prisoners are from, now maybe where we are from, too."

"Planet Prison?" Vittoria asked, perhaps still wondering about bloody windshields, an image I had trouble shaking myself. Not to mention laying there, dying, no one willing to comfort him in any way. Not even a kind word.

"Yeah, a crazy violent place in orbit not far from me and you. We may not live there, but we're in its path."

"Ah, yes. Pulled by the violence?"

"For sure. And pulled to the violence, maybe, willing to do a little of our own."

"But only as the final resort, Rob?"

"Last resort, yeah. But sometimes the last resort is the law."

"How can that be, Rob? Is this one of your riddles?"

"No, unless you think of the death penalty as a riddle."

"I don't think I do. It seems pretty black and white. Do you?"

I resisted the temptation to point out that, 'yes, in America the death penalty was pretty much black and white – white people executing black people who kill white people. Black people who kill black people we're not so hard on. Instead I said, "No, I'm pretty clear on where I stand. But the whole execution business, well, it does leave you thinking. Especially the first time."

"Ah, there have been many for you, right, Rob? Many last nights?"

Many lonely nights, I thought, but decided not to go there. The death house can bring out some pretty basic yearnings, but it would be hard to explain. So I simply said, "Yeah, technically it's a homicide so I attend, make a few notes. Mostly just watch."

"Watch? And say nothing?"

"Not a word, Vittoria. There's not much to say. It's kinda like moving through molasses, everything slow. Guy gets a last meal, kneels there on the floor..."

"Kneels? Like a genuflection?"

"It's not religious, least not as far as I can see. But, yeah, he kneels and eats. Maybe prays. There's no place to sit in the death cell."

"Death cell! Good heavens!"

"Heaven ain't a part of this business, Vittoria. They call it death work. The guy kneels there, puts his tray on the bed, digs in..."

"He has cutlery? Even in the death house?"

It took me a minute to realize that cutlery meant a knife and fork. You lose some of the social graces when you spend a lot of time in prison, especially around the bad guys who kill people and then get killed by the good guys, you allegedly being one of the good guys. At least you hope you're one of the good guys. And you hope like hell you're not watching another murder.

"No, not knives and forks. At least, not metal ones. We give them plastic. Plastic, uh, cutlery. The food's cut up into pieces. They eat what they can. Sometimes share the leftovers with the team."

"Team?"

"The execution team. The people who put him to death." I realized for the first time how odd that must sound. 'The team. My team is the execution squad; the prisoner is the other team, but he's a team of one and a team that has to lose. No contest. That's the rules.'

"Why in the heavens would they share food with their executioners?"

I was glad Vittoria passed by the team business, which made me uncomfortable when I thought about it. Not that sharing food with folks on the other team was much easier to talk about. 'Let's break bread before we break your neck,' I imagined executioners saying back in the day, when the bad guys were hanged.

"There's a strange bond in the death house, Vittoria. I feel it, even though I'm just on the team – uh, in the group, as a kind of prop. You know, an observer."

"And what is it you see, Rob, in your observing role?"

"I see the man eating slowly, solemnly. I see the officers watching him closely. I see the man and the team, uh, the officers, connect, in the sense that this is their night and they are in this together." I didn't want to say their game. "The man is there to die. The guys are there to kill him. Nobody wants things to go wrong, so it's like a dance..."

"A dance? You can sound so strange, Rob. What kind of dance is this?"

I was beginning to feel that this conversation was full of landmines, and maybe that's the way it should be when you talk about a planned killing done under color of law. "Alright, dance is the wrong word. But it's like a script. Everybody has moves to make, and if they make their moves right, things go off without a hitch." I could see Vittoria looked a bit puzzled at the word 'hitch,' so I said, quickly, " Without a problem. It's like nobody wants to face the fact that a cold-blooded killing is the main event." Main event! This sports thing was killing me but I plowed on. "Everybody wants to keep to the schedule and get done."

"Even the man wants to get done?"

He might, I thought, ruefully, knowing full well that a kind of collaboration occurs in the death house; the execution team ready to go, the man pulled along with them, eager to save face, eager to have this nightmare over. It's a kind of collusion that's hard to explain if you haven't been there, so I just stuck to the facts.

"He wants it over, Vittoria. So he follows the script, the team follows the script, and then it's over."

"And everyone goes home, as if nothing happened?"

"No, it's not that simple, but people just keep moving, get through the deal, then go home. And drink, probably."

"Did you drink after the executions?"

"At first? Yeah. I was numb. The drinks went down easy. Scotch. My father's drink. I don't like Scotch and I didn't much like my father, but that's what happened. And it worked. I got good and numb. I almost got lost driving home, then sorta fell into bed when I finally did get home. Woke up the next day wondering what the hell had happened."

Vittoria looked at me curiously. I figured she was thinking about the Scotch and my father; I hadn't mentioned such personal things before. I was relieved she didn't pursue that stuff, at least not now. Instead of prying or probing, she said, "But you knew, of course, what had happened?"

"Yes, I knew, but I had a kind of hollow feeling after it. I mean, the man is helpless at the end. He's locked up in the death house in a bare cell. Everybody's watching him, and ain't nobody about to help him."

"Helpless in the, the death cell?"

"Yes, helpless in the death cell." I flashed on the fact that 'Helpless in the Death Cell' could be some sick flick, inspired by "Sleepless in Seattle" but without the happy ending. I didn't hold onto that thought. "He's got men watching his every move. He's stripped, showered, then fed and killed."

"Fed and killed. Like cattle at the house of slaughter?"

"Yeah, maybe that's right. You know, with cattle at the slaughterhouse, the trick is to arrange the chutes so that the animals don't have a direct route to the kill zone – yeah, that's what it's called sometimes, the kill zone. You want a route to the kill zone that bends, so the cattle can't see where they're going 'til they get there. It's a little like that for the poor bastard in the death house. He can see the chair at the end, but before that, he's caught up in procedures that keep his mind in the present, that keep him focused on the next instant. The chair is at the end of the road but he don't see the end of the road until he's there, and then it's too late to react, I guess. Or maybe too late to take it all in at once. So people just submit, go along. Do what they're told, then die."

"Sad, no? To treat men like cattle?"

And women, I thought, but not so often. Not many women on death row. "Yeah, it is sad. I think the feeling of being trapped in molasses is a reflection of that. You're heavy, you feel dirty. You feel like you smell."

"You feel like you smell?"

"I'm not being poetic here, Vittoria. You feel like there's a stink in the air, and maybe there really is a bad smell, but mostly you sense it. It is a death house, after all, and they – we – used to use the electric chair, which burns..."

"And leaves a stench? Rob, how horrible."

"I'm not sure there is a stench now, Vittoria, but that's how it feels. The needle is better. It looks real painless, but somehow the guy lying there, I don't know, he's completely helpless, like an animal that bares his throat and waits to die."

"It's not like he has a choice, Rob."

"That's right, but we do, and maybe that's what troubles me."

"So you like so many others do not support the capital penalty with all of your heart?"

I smiled, thinking of a pro-death penalty Valentine Card: For the People in Your Life Who Support the Capital Penalty With All of Their Heart! I knew enough to stay away from that conversation. "Oh, no, Vittoria. I don't like the death penalty, but I can live with it. When my world has been rocked, I'm all for it."

"Rob, that sounds so harsh. Not like you, really."

"It is harsh, Vittoria, but a part of me wishes we could take Jake to the death house..."

"Ah, Jake. Our snake. He does..."

"...need a good killing..."

...no, Rob. I was not about to say that. But he does make you want to hurt him, though. Makes me want to hurt him."

I nodded. I admired Vittoria's passion, which every so often trumped her compassion. It rang true, what she said. I wanted to hurt Jake, too. I knew he'd never get the needle but he could damn well pay. I could make him pay. I *would* make him pay. It felt good that I could lock him down in the hole, maybe do a little damage to the smug sonovabitch. The hole is a little like death row but without the death chamber – a dead place, a repository for the living dead. Painful stuff, even if it wasn't the Big Hurt.

I knew we couldn't leave Jake in the hole for long, but we could drop him down there for a spell and put a good scare into him. Who'd know? Who'd believe him? Hardly anyone knows where to find the place, for Christ's sake. Then Jake'd get out and spend the rest of his days in segregation, the modern, antiseptic one – four bare walls for company and non-stop stereophonic hallucinations for entertainment. I mean, people really do go crazy if you leave them in seg long enough, and we pretty much leave the bad actors there for months and even years on end, more than enough time to break a man down. And all legal. And legal long before Abu Ghraib, G'itmo, the whole political deal. This is just everyday cruelty, bread and butter brutality in the prison biz.

People on the outs think they know the drill in segregation. They talk about studies in laboratories, studies with animals, people in sound proof rooms, meting out short, sharp bouts of mental pain. The real deal is a great deal worse. If the guy is weak enough or the stay is long enough, people melt like wax candles, pooling in their own waste, weeping hysterically, yearning to do great bodily harm to themselves to escape the torment. The cells close in; the walls take on a life of their own; voices fill the air. People – one guy called them 'Pod People' – get pulled into the schedule, the routine. "They merge," in Vittoria's words, "with environment around them, it is like they disappear." "Like they're puppets?" I'd asked. "Exactly that," she'd replied, "puppets whose strings are pulled by the prison." I'd forgotten that Vittoria's medical training had included some basic psychiatry.

I'd seen it myself. These puppet people struggle minute to minute to hold onto their sanity, which is a crazy thing in itself – what's a sane puppet? – and then, one day, they just let go, like they're *wanting* to lose it, to go crazy, to get so far out of their heads they won't have to suffer any more.

Eyes. Talk about eyes in cell windows. In seg you got some guys with nothing but empty fucking eye sockets. Empty eye sockets! Think about that. Raw looking; trust me. Medical care in here don't include cosmetic surgery. Tore their own eyes out of their sorry heads to get some relief. Figure maybe, if they can't see the world, the world can't hurt them. Blindness is bliss, that sort of thing. But it don't work that way. One guy *ate* both his eyes, one on Friday, the other on Saturday. Come Monday, he was even crazier. And crazed. Long gone. Now, that guy's extreme. The eating part makes him unusual; not that he took out his own eyes. To quote Vittoria, "self-enucleation, or the forcible taking of one's own modality of vision in response to dire circumstances is not uncommon in penal institutions." With the guys marooned in seg, you got faces at the door but nobody's home. Their daily existence is a dire fucking circumstance.

There's even more strange stuff in seg but the truly odd thing is how all this comes to seem normal to the staff, the men and women in the trenches, me included. Vittoria's an exception; she's one of those folks who manage to care 24-7, day in and day out. But Vittoria is, well, Vittoria. Someone who cares for the dead. Really cares. A class act, that lady. For most of us, the horror gradually becomes a part of how we look at the world, and maybe don't look too closely at ourselves. Shows you we can do anything long enough and figure it must be normal; something's wrong with the person, maybe, but not the world – not the seg unit, home to terrible tortures we take for granted. Not the seg unit *we* run. And seg is a place *you* should run from, run as far and as fast as you can. If you can. But, see, Jake and the others back there, they can't run. They can't move. They are trapped, and in a sick way, it is a beautiful sight to behold, all this suffering they so richly deserve.

So, when you get right down to it, segregation can be hell. And I'm willing to get right down to it, especially for the likes of Jake the Snake. He's living in Daunte's Inferno, burning alive for the betrayal of a man who tried to live in this hell and made the mistake of trusting him. And really, I'm OK with all this, which tells me that Planet Prison may not be as foreign to me as I'd like to think.

ABOUT THE AUTHOR

Robert Johnson is a professor of justice, law and society at American University, editor and publisher of BleakHouse Publishing, and an award-winning author of books and articles on crime and punishment, including works of social science, law, poetry, and fiction. He has testified or provided expert affidavits on capital and other criminal cases in many venues, including US state and federal courts, the U.S. Congress, and the European Commission of Human Rights. He is best known for his book, *Death Work: A Study of the Modern Execution Process*, which won the Outstanding Book Award of the Academy of Criminal Justice Sciences. Johnson is a Distinguished Alumnus of the Nelson A. Rockefeller College of Public Affairs and Policy, University at Albany, State University of New York.

ABOUT THE ARTISTS

Sonia Tabriz (Cover Art & Text Design) graduated from American University (2010) *summa cum laude* with University Honors, with a B.A. in Law and Society and a B.A. in Psychology. She received the Outstanding Scholarship at the Undergraduate Level award for her award-winning works of fiction, legal commentaries, artwork, presentations, university-wide accolades, and academic achievement. Tabriz received a J.D. degree from The George Washington University Law School (2013), where she was a merit scholar and served as a Writing Fellow as well as Editor-in-Chief of the *Public Contract Law Journal*. Tabriz, the Managing Editor of BleakHouse Publishing, will be joining a firm in Washington, D.C. to practice government contracts law.

Liz Calka (Cover Design) is an award-winning designer and photographer with a degree in Visual Media and Graphic Design from American University. As Art Director at BleakHouse Publishing, she has designed covers and layouts for a number of

BleakHouse publications including books and magazines. She also created and maintains the BleakHouse website.

Rachel Ternes (illustrations) is an honors undergraduate student at American University majoring in psychology and minoring French and studio arts. Her passion for creating art is rivaled only by her interest in using her artistic skills to promote causes of social justice. As Chief Creative Officer for BleakHouse Publishing, Ternes designs visuals for press releases and publicity, and contributes to the visual design and illustration of publications.

Commentaries

Prison Murder, Up Close and Savage:
A Collage of Commentaries on *Miller's Revenge*

(Reprinted from *Tacenda Literary Magazine*, 2011)

Miller's Revenge
A novel by Robert Johnson
Brown Paper Publishing, 2010
(BleakHouse Publishing Reprint Edition, 2013)

Revenge Hurts
By Tim Gallivan

The Real Deal
By Charles Huckelbury

A Review and Commentary
By Kerry Myers

Revenge Hurts:
A Review of *Miller's Revenge*
By Tim Gallivan

Miller's Revenge, a novel written by Robert Johnson, transports the reader into a sordid place—an American prison. In a narrative describing one long day marked by lethal violence and other atavisms, the reader confronts a few of the sickening realities that are fixtures in the lives of many prisoners. The protagonist, Detective Robert Miller, is employed in an archetypal penal facility, a place in which murder, rape, and suicidal behavior are looming possibilities on any given day. While "Planet Prison" may seem completely alien to anyone who has never visited, this brutal world quickly becomes the norm for those incarcerated or employed within its confines.

From the onset of *Miller's Revenge*, it is apparent that fear is the driving emotion in the prison. Absolutely no one is safe, and one has the sense that there are only two options for the prison's inmates: dominate or be dominated. The Corrections Officers (COs), who are ostensibly charged with maintaining order, often fail to stop the violence they witness. In one of the novel's most gripping scenes, nearby COs fail to act while a young inmate is stabbed and strangled to death on a prison bus. The COs' inaction reinforces the profound instability and pervasive fear of the prison environment.

Certainly, prisoners can try to escape the hell that is prison by seeking the comforts of routine. Miller describes how most life sentence prisoners, colloquially called lifers, want nothing more than to avoid violence and danger and strive to live "in the moment." Many lifers, we learn, establish elaborate and detailed routines so that they can ignore the harsh realities of their environment and achieve some semblance of accomplishment on a daily basis. If all prisoners adopted this mentality, then prison violence would be a rarity. There are, however, "outlaws" in prison: those who want to steal the relative peace and comfort that some prisoners have simply because they are filled with hate and anger. It is these individuals who make prison a jungle.

For this reason, it seems that no one can be unscathed by violence and pain while incarcerated. Knowing this, it becomes rather difficult to judge an inmate's crimes because it is often impossible to determine whether he or she was acting defensively. Even if the conditions do not seem to lend themselves to a clear-cut case of defense, one must always consider the effects that a generally violent atmosphere have on an individual. In response to the constant dangers of the prison environment, an individual might (understandably) become paranoid and excessively defensive.

Hence, Daunte McFadden's murder of Jamal Jordan cannot easily be condemned as cold-blooded homicide because it took place in the unique prison environment. It is certainly arguable that McFadden believed he was in mortal danger because he was called to the gym when it was not his day to attend a basketball game. While most individuals in the free world would not make such a leap, the environment that exists within the incarcerated world makes such leaps necessary for survival.

Although McFadden acknowledged that his information may not have been completely accurate (and Jordan did not actually intend to kill him), he believed that he would die if he did not respond to his perceived threat. As McFadden understood the situation, "If the word is out that I'm a target, then I am a target. Either the word is true and serious bodily harm is set on my ass. Or the word is false but if I don't act — take somebody down — people think I'm lame. Then some other motherfucka will take me down 'cause he think I'm an easy score." When Miller asks McFadden why he could not just walk away, McFadden replies that he had nowhere to go; in prison, there is no refuge from violence.

Even John J. Gibb's (or "Jake the Snake's") behavior presents complexities, making the point that in prison, violence "ain't no clean thing." Things simply aren't black and white. Gibb was a tortured soul, caught in the unrelenting grips of unrequited love. Presumably, this would be an extremely painful ordeal in prison, where love is a scarce commodity that few have the privilege of feeling. Moreover, for Gibb, love was a passionate, all-consuming sentiment that seemed to strip him of his sanity.

By the novel's end, Miller's view of things has unfortunately become jaded. He comes to relish the prospect of putting violent prisoners in the arcane "hole" that lingers on as a relic of cruelty in the prison's dungeon, somehow unsatisfied with the standard brutal option of placing prisoners in solitary confinement. The thought of prisoners suffering greatly in the hole is genuinely gratifying to Miller, whose humane sentiments, clear at the beginning of the story, are fading with the dying light of this long prison day. By day's end, the prison has finally taken a hold over Miller mentally and emotionally, and he, too, has become prison property.

Tim Gallivan graduated *summa cum laude* and with University Honors in Political Science from American University. Gallivan is attending the University of Virginia School of Law, where he serves on the Law Review.

The Real Deal
A Review of *Miller's Revenge*
By Charles Huckelbury

Only rarely does a reader encounter an author with the imagination and technical skills to animate his subject vividly enough to evoke a physical response in the reader. This is especially true when the author has no personal experience with the events he or she is describing. Robert Johnson is such an author, and his latest work of fiction, *Miller's Revenge,* is precisely that kind of evocative tale.

We meet Robert Miller, the novel's first-person narrator, immediately after Daunte McFadden has killed Jamal Jordan in a maximum-security prison in Baltimore. Miller is the cop assigned to the prison and responsible for investigating all homicides and ancillary other offenses. This is no whodunit; we know immediately who did it and where. The challenge Robert Johnson presents is to understand the why part of the equation.

Miller, quite naturally, brings a cynic's eye to his thankless job, necessary to inoculate him against the horrors that haunt the prison. But that cynicism doesn't disable his human response to the misery he sees daily. Early in the book he tells us, "It's a grim business, this dying in prison." This understated eloquence is of a piece with Miller's unconcealed sorrow for the human destruction he encounters and compassion for its victims. And yet he remains the cop with a cop's attitude: "Some call it snitching. I call it. . . doing the right thing." Thus the line between con and cop remains intact, adding to the objectivity of what Miller tells us.

Using Daunte's killing of Jamal as the vehicle, Miller gives us a guided tour of how maximum-security prisons operate, acknowledging pressures and circumstances that most readers will never comprehend. He discusses the mutually beneficial collusion between guards and cons, technically proscribed by prison rules but casually disregarded as an existential reality. His depiction of the modern prison as an incarnation of the plantation will produce nods of agreement by anyone who has ever walked the yard or been inside a cell, and his criticism of the drug war's disastrous human costs acknowledges the role that battle has had in making prisons even more dangerous.

Miller's narrative is not, however, unremittingly bleak. Johnson also gives us Vittoria Simone, the medical examiner who plays off Miller's cynicism in order to remind us that the dead men she encounters were once loved and valued as human beings, no matter what kind of self-inflicted destruction brought them to prison. In a skillful counterstroke,

Miller tells her that he believes instead that some men in prison had "never been loved ...even as children."

As accurate as the topical and relevant ethnography is, what impresses most about this book is Johnson's incredible grasp of detail, from the appearance and smell of a burned-out cell to the technique used by Duante to kill Jamal. Most prisoners, including this reviewer, have a tendency to disregard prison-based fiction as irretrievably flawed if not written by one of us. Gaping holes in both philosophy and detail frequently emerge, simply from a lack of experience or insight.

Not so in Robert Johnson's version. If I didn't know better, I would automatically assume that Johnson had been there, done that, and gotten the tee shirt to prove it. Indeed, his description of the murder inside the prison's gym is eerily similar to a murder I, along with 240 other men, witnessed over thirty years ago, including the weapons and tactics of the combatants. Johnson even puts the correct jargon in his characters' mouths and reminds us that the prisoners don't "really live here like human beings," a position validated by the brutality of the murder itself. More to the point, the novel's denouement validates the title and prison maxim that what goes around comes around.

Robert Johnson is a masterful stylist with an anthropologist's grasp of his subject, engaging the reader as a participant-observer inside the unforgiving and refracted world of maximum security. Nowhere else have I encountered such a remarkable ability to describe the hopeless failure than massive incarceration has become, combined with an experienced, albeit jaundiced, view of human depravity and low expectations in an environment where life is lived according to the lowest common denominator. This book is a significant contribution to the discussion of social policy and the elephant sitting in the living room of every state's budget crisis. The genre is fiction, but the story it tells is terrifyingly real.

Charles Huckelbury was recently paroled after serving thirty-eight consecutive years in prison. He is on the editorial board of the *Journal of Prisoners on Prisons* and the winner of four PEN American awards for both fiction and nonfiction. He is the author of two volumes of poetry, *Tales from the Purple Penguin* and *Distant Thunder.*

Miller's Revenge
By Robert Johnson

A Review and Commentary
By Kerry Myers

The first significant impression this book makes to a reader is the use of soliloquies and dialogue that seem equally competent for a screenplay as it does for a novel. It was easy to imagine the main character as an actor, spotlit in an archaic, dark and dank stone edifice called prison, thinking out loud about the nature of his job. The reader is present to his thoughts on prison and the people who inhabit it, and the system that builds and fills places packed with people sentenced to serve more time than God ever intended, people manufacturing lives and futures out of nothing.

The nature of the main character's first soliloquy, one that questions the very efficacy of public policy that makes little distinction and discourages discretion between those caught in the vortex of fear mongering and expediency, is all the more cinematic or theatric because the thinker is part of the system, a public safety investigator assigned to investigate crimes in the very stereotypical, multi-tiered, cell house-style, 19th or early 20th century state prison.

Interesting dialogue with a moderately young, female Italian medical examiner, someone without the unique American sense of crime and punishment, and who thus is just naive enough to ask relevant questions, feel the collective societal loss that warehousing prisoners creates, and show compassion for the humanity of each "victim" that finds himself on her cold, sterile table in the morgue, establishes the writer's uncertainty and even disdain for what the system has become even in his time within it.

Robert Johnson, through his alter ego Rob Miller, questions and examines the effects that hopelessness, despair and the innate survival instinct have on men confined in harsh conditions, stripped of dignity and subjected to daily assaults on their humanity. What, he wonders, is the damage to the human psyche? He senses the prison itself as the "beast" that steals lives, steals souls, steals whatever it can from whoever it can, even those whose job it is to "guard" the inmates by ensuring that the perimeter is secure and that clearing the regular counts protect the public safety.

Johnson describes a prison much different than the Louisiana State Penitentiary at Angola, where 80 percent of its prisoners live in dormitories and have regular jobs and are involved in a plethora of organized, sanctioned activities that occupy their time and their minds. But like the walled fortress he describes, which still exists in many places in the country, Angola is still a "beast" confining 5,200 prisoners, 76 percent of whom are serving life without parole and 62 percent who are now over 40 years old. They live, work and play each day in a large "bowl," the sides of which most will never successfully scale to see over the rim to the free world outside.

Through Rob Miller, Johnson creates a palpable portrait of the "beast" and the society that lives within. Trading and bartering, with commissary items and with people too mentally weak to stave off the assault of fear, is the commerce that oils the engine of this society. In many ways life in this prison, and all prisons, is evolutionary, the natural selection of leaders, workers, soldiers and those that become property. It is reminiscent of *Animal Farm* and the societal structure that evolves through natural order. Fear, violence, paranoia and a mob mentality are as integral to the *Animal Farm* paradigm as they are to prison life.

Johnson presents Daunte McFadden as a flawed, but totally human character with the same hopes, dreams and needs as anyone. Unlike most people, and like most prisoners, Daunte's life was dysfunctional, his wants and needs disordered, thus his choices led him to prison. But his humanity is not completely gone. He wants to survive, he understands the "beast" and how it preys on the weak. He knows the code of the life he lives and, to his demise, he trusted someone, a basic human trait that tells us we have value to another person. Rob Miller understands that the paranoia and fear perpetuated in prison, and specifically to the circumstances of Daunte. Manipulated by information from another prisoner that there is a "hit" out on him, the perceptive truth of Daunte's world is that he is backed into a corner and left little choice about what needs to be done in order to survive. Daunte simply wanted to live, and so he took the only course of action known to him. Rob Miller did not condone but did understand the deeply running rivers that were at work.

The book is an indictment of sort of the way the nation deals with its prisoners, even those convicted of violent crimes.

The subliminal programming term "violent criminal" often used by politicians, law enforcement and the media is completely misleading. Many people in prison are convicted of violent crimes but are not career violent criminals or perpetually violent. In fact, most people convicted of a violent crime are not career violent criminals. With the exception of the pathological personality, the truly mentally ill, and the career violent criminal, most people convicted of a violent crime made poor, life-changing choices in a difficult or stressful situation.

Johnson suggests that the policy of warehousing people, human beings, in hollow places of despair and hopelessness actually perpetuates the darkest part of society, one it would rather see in the reflection of a mirror than entwined in their real life. "It occurred to me, not for the first time, that human animals just don't live well in captivity," Rob Miller thought to himself. The punishment society metes out and the effectiveness of that punishment can be glimpsed in that statement. When is punishment no longer punishment but revenge? When does the effect of the punishment wane and the punished become either a cowered animal or an overly aggressive predator? When does the benefit for the public safety end if risk is no longer a factor, and the use of resources to continue useless punishment becomes immoral?

Miller sarcastically examines a commonly held misconception, born of societal ignorance of prisoners and public policy, when he speaks about homosexuality in prison, saying, "... it was better to let the men go at each other - and especially at the wayward teens sprinkled in courtesy of the drug war, some doing life without - than to subject prisoners to the horrors of pornography." Most prisons banned "shot books," slang for pornography, a decade ago in response to a growing public fear of sex offenders, thinking that *Playboy*, *Hustler* and other prurient magazines would exacerbate the problem and create a hostile work environment for the growing cadre of female correctional officers. In fact, the banning of these magazines has had an opposite effect. In Tennessee, the incidences of inmate sex offenses actually went up in the year after the "shot book" ban went into effect.

Societal attitudes are again subjected to critical commentary when Miller thinks to himself that, "at least with zoos, people bring their families to visit and have to be told not to feed the captives. Most of us would just as soon see the convicts starve, and we sure as hell wouldn't bring our families to see the carnage."

Robert Johnson does not advocate that prisons are unneeded or unnecessary. Rather, he indicts the system and the policies that perpetuate it by preferring to put people, humans, away forever in cages, out of sight, out of mind, buried somewhere where the rest of society does not have to deal with the real problems or the real ugliness. "I don't like to think of myself as a vengeful man," Miller says to himself after ensuring that Daunte's killer is put into the worst conditions in the prison designed to break his will and his mind, "but at times the hopelessness all around me in prison makes me burn with resentment, makes me want to lash out." If this can happen to a person in law enforcement, someone working inside the system, consider what Johnson is saying about those confined inside? What hopelessness does society continue to heap upon prisoners serving life sentences, many of whom are first offenders? What resentment does the system create when those trapped inside feel helpless to find redemption? It's a question "Miller's Revenge" asks but does not resolve—very deliberately.

Kerry Myers was born in New Orleans, Louisiana and grew up in suburban Jefferson Parish. He holds a degree in communications and had a successful career in the private sector, spending eight years with an industrial firm in sales, marketing and producing training programs. He was convicted of second degree murder in 1990 and confined at Angola State Prison, though he has and continues to maintain his innocence. He joined *The Angolite* staff as a writer in 1996, and became editor in 2001 after the departure of longtime editor Wilbert Rideau. During his tenure as editor the magazine has gone through a redesign, won three APEX Awards for Excellence in Magazine and Journal Writing and a Thurgood Marshall Journalism Award. *The Angolite* magazine has a subscriber base of approximately 1,200 both domestically and internationally, reaching all 50 states and six foreign countries.

Praise for Miller's Revenge

Miller's Revenge is a remarkable novel. Its author, an academic social psychologist and long-time professor at American University who has studied prison life and executions, here inhabits in fiction the grim world he has been studying. The result is a novel that not only presents believable characters in a deeply disturbing setting; it conveys a lot of truth as well.

Jeffrey H. Reiman
William Fraser McDowell Professor of Philosophy
American University
Washington, DC

"Robert Johnson has done it again! The book is his canvas and his words are his paint. His stories are mesmerizing landscapes that capture us and take us places we've never been. He is a true poetic version of a film director, Tim Burton, masterfully bringing his stories to life. In "Miller's Revenge," Johnson takes us on a rollercoaster of emotions and invites our senses to attune themselves to the peculiar frequency of the American prison. As we read we lose ourselves, and in that moment, we stride through the convict's world. Each step is a step closer to their world – we smell what they smell, touch what they touch, hear the sounds they hear. Every description intoxicates our senses and we find ourselves pulled in to the pages of this story, examining each section in detail, almost pixel by pixel (to think in terms of imagery). Anyone looking for a great read, a few good laughs, and a refreshing outlook on the necessary evil of our penal system must read this book. You are in for a great ride!"

Ania Dobrzanska
U.S. Department of Justice
Office of Justice Programs
Bureau of Justice Assistance

CPSIA information can be obtained at www.ICGtesting.com
Printed in the USA
BVOW01s0015300913

332450BV00007B/36/P